ONE SU
AFTERNOON

Tilly Bagshawe is the internationally bestselling author of eight previous novels. A teenage single mother at 17, Tilly won a place at Cambridge University and took her baby daughter with her. She went on to enjoy a successful career in The City before becoming a writer. As a journalist, Tilly contributed regularly to the *Sunday Times*, *Daily Mail* and *Evening Standard* before following in the footsteps of her sister Louise and turning her hand to novels.

Tilly's first book, *Adored*, was a smash hit on both sides of the Atlantic and she hasn't looked back since. Tilly and her family divide their time between their homes in Los Angeles and their beach house on Nantucket Island.

Also by Tilly Bagshawe

Adored
Showdown
Do Not Disturb
Flawless
Fame
Scandalous
Friends & Rivals
The Inheritance

One Christmas Morning (A Swell Valley Short Story)

Sidney Sheldon's Mistress of the Game
Sidney Sheldon's After the Darkness
Sidney Sheldon's Angel of the Dark
Sidney Sheldon's The Tides of Memory
Sidney Sheldon's Chasing Tomorrow

ONE SUMMER'S AFTERNOON

HARPER

Harper
An imprint of HarperCollins*Publishers*
77-85 Fulham Palace Road
London, W6 8JB

www.harpercollins.co.uk

This paperback edition 2014
1

First published in Great Britain by
HarperCollins*Publishers* 2013

Copyright © Tilly Bagshawe 2013

Tilly Bagshawe asserts the moral right to
be identified as the author of this work

A catalogue record for this book is
available from the British Library

ISBN: 978-0-00-812118-1

Set in Meridien by Palimpsest Book Production Limited,
Falkirk, Stirlingshire

MIX
Paper from
responsible sources
FSC **FSC™ C007454**
www.fsc.org

MONDAY

'All right, so let's run through it again. Who's going to open the batting with Will?'

The five men considered this all-important question in the beer garden of Fittlescombe's prettiest pub, The Fox. This Saturday was the big match, an annual cricketing fixture between Fittlescombe and the neighbouring village of Brockhurst. Dating back more than a hundred and fifty years, the Swell Valley cricket match was older than the Ashes, and every bit as hotly contested. For the last six years in a row, shamingly, Brockhurst had trounced the home team. Indeed, almost since the match's inception, Fittlescombe had been perceived as something of a gentle-manly shambles, gracious losers in the great tradition of affable, British sporting failures. The village had produced only two county players in the last century, in comparison with Brockhurst's six, and no Test cricketers at all (Brockhurst could boast two). But this year the men of Fittlescombe were confident the tables would be turned, thanks in no small part to the return to their ranks of William Nutley, a brilliant batsman whom many locals considered good enough to play at county level. Will had grown up in the village, but his family had moved away a few years back, after old man Nutley lost the family fortune in a string of bad investments and was forced to sell his gorgeous Elizabethan manor house. But now, aged twenty-two, Will was back, living modestly in a rundown farmworker's cottage, and playing better than ever.

'It should be one of the older lads. Someone steadying, to calm the boy's nerves.'

It was George Blythe, the local carpenter and Fittlescombe's captain, who made this observation, but it was greeted by universal nods and murmurs of assent from his table mates – namely Dylan Pritchard Jones, the handsome young art teacher at St Hilda's School in the village; Gabe Baxter, a local farmer and handy fielder with a first-class bowling arm; Timothy Wright, a retired stockbroker who lived in the village and who in his youth had been a star bowler at Eton; and Frank Bannister, the sweet-natured church organist, who was frankly an appalling cricketer but was far too nice a person to be kicked off the team. The Fittlescombe XI ranged in age from fourteen (Seb Harwich was coming home from school for the match) to sixty-five-year-old Timothy, and the levels of ability were equally diverse. Not all of the players had been able to make it to tonight's get-together at The Fox. But all had agreed that the five men present would settle on a batting and bowling order, as well as arranging a schedule for the week's practices. The key question at issue, however, was whom to pair with Will Nutley. Everybody knew that, while Will was their great white hope, he was also prone to terrible nerves. Especially when playing in front of his beautiful ex-girlfriend, Emma Harwich, who was sure to be there on Saturday supporting her brother. One silly mistake, one lapse in concentration on Will's part, and all Fittlescombe's long-cherished hopes would be dashed. The choice of batting partner was crucial.

'I vote Tim,' said Gabe Baxter. Blond and stocky, like a handsome pit-bull terrier, Gabe was considered the sexiest player of the tournament, closely followed by the good-looking but terribly vain Dylan Pritchard Jones. 'You're our safest pair of hands. And you've known Will forever.'

Timothy Wright smiled ruefully. Bald and paunchy, with a permanently red nose and cheeks latticed with broken red veins after a lifetime of hard drinking, Timothy was *not* one of Fittlescombe's heart-throbs. 'I'm flattered, dear boy, but an opening batsman I am not. I'm afraid I'm very much a one-trick pony.'

'Lionel, then?' said George Blythe, the thin and wiry village captain.

Lionel Green, owner of Green's Books on the high street, was the next oldest player after Timothy at fifty-seven, and a competent, if not spectacular, batsman.

'I think he'd be a better bet,' said Timothy. 'He should steady the lad's nerves. Although the very best thing would be to think of a way to stop the Harwich girl from coming at all.'

'I doubt you'll succeed at that,' Dylan Pritchard Jones said archly. At thirty-two years old, with a thick mop of curly hair and twinkly, lapis-blue eyes, Dylan was considered almost as much of a catch as Gabe Baxter; although, like Gabe, he was spoken for, married to the patient and lovely Maisie. 'Emma Harwich could give Tatiana Flint-Hamilton a run for her money when it comes to loving the cameras. There's bound to be a ton of press here on Saturday. She won't miss a chance to get her pretty little face in the papers.'

Local teen Emma Harwich had been signed to a London modelling agency last year, since when her career had taken off exponentially. A few months ago Emma was named as the new face of Burberry, and was rapidly eclipsing Tatiana Flint-Hamilton as Fittlescombe's most famous beauty. Emma and Will Nutley had briefly dated a few years ago. But that was back when Emma was an unknown, and Will had expected to inherit a not-so-small fortune.

'Shhh,' Timothy Wright hissed. 'He's coming.'

Will Nutley emerged from the bar back out into the garden, carrying a tray laden with beers. Six foot five, with broad shoulders and enormous hands and feet, Will had been nicknamed BFG at school. With his red hair, freckles and big amber eyes, fringed with lashes as long and thick as a camel's, Will was not what one would call classically hand-some. But he was funny and self-effacing and blessed with immense charm – what his father Donald called his 'likability factor'. It was this that had helped him find work as a recruitment consultant, despite his conspicuous lack of A-levels or degree. A country boy at heart, Will loathed his city job, but he was smart enough to be grateful for the income it afforded him. At least he earned enough to live in Fittlescombe and commute.

Will lived for long warm summer evenings like this one, spent with friends in the idyllic garden of his favourite pub. Picking his way unsteadily along the winding stone path, bordered on either side by towering hollyhocks and foxgloves, he made his way to the large table by the pond. Overhung by a hundred-year-old willow tree, whose gnarled trunk leaned towards the water and whose long green fronds provided shelter for the dragonflies that darted across the lily pads like kamikaze bombers, this was the farthest table from the playground and the distracting whoops and shrieks of local children.

'You took your time,' said Dylan Pritchard Jones

good-naturedly, relieving Will of the tray and handing round the heavy pints of warm, half-spilled beer. 'Hey, I was only joking,' he added, catching Will's stricken face.

'It's not you,' said Will, sitting down heavily at the table. His team-mates exchanged worried glances.

'W-what's the matter?' asked Frank Bannister, the organist. 'Has something happened?'

'You look like you've seen a ghost, mate,' added Gabe Baxter.

'I was just talking to Danny,' said Will gloomily. Danny Jenner was The Fox's landlord and a Fittlescombe institution. With the honourable exceptions of Graham the barber and Mrs Martel the chemist, Danny Jenner was the biggest gossip in the Swell Valley. 'You won't believe who Brockhurst have brought in at the last moment.'

Five beer glasses thudded down on the table simultaneously.

'Who?' the men asked in unison.

'Only Santiago de la bloody Cruz,' said Will, putting his head in his hands. 'Can you believe it?'

They couldn't. Santiago de la Cruz was a world-famous name in cricket, and for all the wrong reasons. Preposterously handsome, with olive skin, hair as glossy and blue-black as a raven's, and a proud aquiline nose that gave him a predatory air, Santiago had been born to an Argentine mother and English father. Raised in Buenos Aires, Santiago was at least as well known for his advertising contracts and playboy antics as he was for his prowess as a fast bowler. Argentina not being a Test-cricketing nation, de la Cruz had transplanted himself to England, where he'd promptly been snapped up to play for the Sussex county team. Not since Imran Khan's captaincy had cricket in Sussex had such a high profile. Ticket sales had gone through the roof, with a

huge surge in female fans flocking to the stands at Hove to
catch a glimpse of their idol, with his soulful eyes, so dark
they were almost black, and his sensual mouth, set in a
semi-permanent expression of sardonic amusement. It was
well known that Santiago had ambitions to play for England,
although, at thirty-one and without an international cap to
his name, that looked like a long shot. In the meantime,
however, he already made more in sponsorship deals than
international stars like Freddie Flintoff and Kevin Pietersen,
thanks to his good looks and media savvy alone.

'Are you sure?' asked Timothy Wright. 'I think Danny
must have been pulling your leg. The rules are quite clear:
all players for both teams *must* live in their respective villages.
Santiago de la Cruz doesn't live in Brockhurst. He lives in
Brighton.'

'Not any more, he doesn't,' said Will. 'He's rented that
thatched place on Woodbury Lane. Moved in yesterday,
apparently, on a one-year lease.'

'That's outrageous!' said Gabe.

'Shipping in professionals like that – it's bloody cheating
is what it is,' agreed Dylan.

'It's not cheating,' Will said reasonably. 'They don't have
to confirm their final line-up till Wednesday.'

'It's completely against the spirit of the thing,' chipped in
Timothy Wright. 'Typical bloody Brockhurst.'

Will shrugged. 'Whatever. He's here, he's playing and he's
opening the bowling for Brockhurst on Saturday. Charlie
Kingham was overheard at the Black Swan last night,
boasting about it. Apparently, the landlord over there's
running a book on how many overs it'll take de la Cruz to
take my wicket.'

'Are they, now?' As captain, George Blythe felt the onus
was on him to defend Will's reputation, and by extension

Fittlescombe's chances. 'Well, don't you worry about it, William. Pride comes before a fall. De la Cruz is such a peacock, I expect he'll be too busy worrying about his hair and make-up to see you coming.'

They all laughed, except for poor Will.

Santiago de la Cruz's good looks worried him at least as much as his famous rival's bowling arm.

Will had been banking on using this summer's cricket match to win back the heart of his first love, Emma Harwich.

If I could score a century, and take home the Swell Valley cup for Fittlescombe, maybe she'd start to fancy me again, he'd argued to himself, night after night for almost a year. But now, with cricket's answer to David Beckham swooping in to seize the limelight at the last moment, what possible chance did he have?

It was unlike Will Nutley to hate anybody. But at that moment, listening to the reassuring platitudes of his team-mates, Will came close to hating Santiago de la Cruz.

Santiago de la Cruz flipped open his vintage Hermès suitcase and lifted out a stack of perfectly pressed, sky-blue linen shirts. Karen, his PA, had done a stellar job packing up his penthouse flat on the front in Brighton and installing him here, at Wheelers Cottage. He'd arrived yesterday to find his bed made, his fridge stocked and his Sky Sports fully operational. Other than hanging up his shirts, there wasn't a thing for him to do.

Santiago had never understood what possessed otherwise intelligent men to hire useless, leggy blondes as personal assistants. He was as much a fan of leggy blondes as the next man. But all PAs worth their salt were over fifty and a solid 80 per cent battleaxe. Karen was two stone over-weight, wore surgical stockings come rain or shine and had blisters on her hands as tough as barnacles after a lifetime's heavy lifting. She'd made Santiago's move to Brockhurst a dream. A good thing, as he'd been having nightmares about it since the day his agent had persuaded him to sign on the dotted line.

'You'll love it,' the agent had assured him, over a wildly expensive lunch at the Dorchester that he would no doubt bill Santiago for later. 'That part of the country's alive with hot chicks.'

'It's the middle of fucking nowhere,' Santiago had grumbled.

'Who cares?' The agent grinned. 'You won't want to leave.'

'I loathe the countryside.'

'No you don't. You love it. Which is why you're gonna make the perfect face of the Best of Britain Hotel Group.'

And there was the rub. Santiago's year-long prison sentence in some godforsaken Sussex village was going to earn him a cool two million pounds in sponsorship from a leisure consortium that specialized in five-star country-house hotels. They'd originally wanted him to tour the country as an 'ambassador' for their various different properties, but as a county player Santiago had to stay in Sussex. Brilliantly, his agent had brokered a deal whereby his client would spend a year in a chocolate-box thatched house in Brockhurst, home of English cricket. He would play in the famous Swell Valley One-Day Match, which in recent years had become almost as popular a society fixture as the Boat Race or the Cartier Polo. In return, the leisure group would have use of the house, and the coveted de la Cruz image, for various promotional shoots and events, all endorsing their 'Best of Britain' brand. And Santiago would plug their hotels relentlessly at every possible opportunity.

It had seemed like a no-brainer at the time – money for

nothing. He could still play for the county, still commute to London for weekends in the off season. But, now that he was actually here, his heart sank. The house was picture perfect, but it was the sort of house a wealthy grandmother might retire to, all low ceilings and beams and leaded-light windows. Santiago had already cracked his head twice. The whole place made him feel horribly claustrophobic. As for the wall-to-wall stunning women Santiago's agent had promised him, so far he'd seen nothing but a couple of middle-aged village shopkeepers and a gaggle of overweight teenagers, who had pointed and stared at him as they loitered around Brockhurst's only bus stop yesterday, as if he were an animal in a zoo.

After putting the last of his shirts into the heavy Victorian chest of drawers by the window, he opened the latch and stuck his head outside. The views, at least, were fabulous. From his bedroom window, Santiago looked over his pretty cottage garden to the glorious Swell Valley beyond. Startlingly green fields sloped down to the River Swell, a wide, glinting swathe of silver, snaking its way along the valley floor. On the far side of the river, the South Downs rose up dramatically like great, benevolent giants. The grass on the hills was a paler green than in the valley – almost grey, in fact – and crisscrossed with bright white paths that had been etched into the chalk over thousands of years. Only one building was visible, at the foot of the Downs close to where Fittlescombe village lay hidden from view, folded between two hills. It was a medieval hall house, probably a large farm originally, and it stood surrounded by its own orchards. Curious, Santiago picked up his 'Best of Britain' binoculars from the dressing table (his sponsors had provided him with a number of twee, country-themed gifts, including walking sticks with carved pheasants' heads on the top, a fly-fishing rod and an engraved hip flask, presumably for use on fictional shooting weekends) and zoomed in on the house.

The first thing he noticed was that the binoculars were superb. He had a perfect view of the house and garden, and was even able to zoom in on the roses climbing up the brickwork. The second thing he noticed was the front door opening and an incredibly pretty blonde in a tiny floral bikini, emerging into the garden. She was carrying a bath towel and a magazine and, despite being barefoot and (presumably) alone in her own garden, she carried herself as if she had an audience, with the haughty, self-satisfied bearing of the very young and very beautiful.

Spreading out the towel, she proceeded immediately to remove her bikini top, revealing a pair of small but perfectly formed breasts, like two apples dipped in caramel.

Santiago let out a long, low whistle. Now that really *was* the best of Britain, or at a minimum the best of Brockhurst. Would she be at the match on Saturday? he wondered. Surely she was bound to be. It wasn't as if there was anything else to do around here.

He closed the window and went downstairs in search of a cold gin and tonic, feeling mildly cheered.

Perhaps his agent would turn out to have been right after all.

The Swell Valley was starting to look up.

TUESDAY

'Oh, for fuck's sake!'

Penelope Harwich stared down at the blackened chicken casserole, so badly burned it probably couldn't even be identified from its dental records, and ran her hands through her hair in despair.

'Why didn't the bloody bipper go off?'

This last question was addressed to Sebastian, Penny's fourteen-year-old son, who was hunched over the kitchen table at Woodside Hall, deep in his Nintendo 3DS.

'It did,' he said without looking up. 'I turned it off.'

'Why?' wailed Penny.

'Because it was annoying,' said Seb, reasonably.

'Yes, but why didn't you come and get me? I set it so I'd remember to take the lunch out of the oven!'

'Well I didn't know that, did I?' said Seb, reluctantly turning off his game and pushing open the kitchen door, to allow the smoke to escape. 'You set that thing all the time – to remember to call granny, to remember to do the ironing, to remember some other thing you're supposed to remember.'

Penny groaned. She wished this weren't true. That she

didn't muddle through her life like a victim of early-onset Alzheimer's, barely able to brush her own hair or make a cup of tea without some sort of outside assistance. But, ever since her divorce last year (since her husband, Paul, had left her on their twentieth wedding anniversary, for a man, admitting to a gay double life that Penny had had literally no suspicion of whatsoever), she'd lost so much confidence she barely trusted herself to remember her own name.

'I think we'd better leave this in the garden for a bit. Till it stops, you know, smoking,' said Seb.

Watching her lovely, kind, capable fourteen-year-old son slip on her oven gloves and carry the charred mess outside, Penny Harwich felt poleaxed with guilt. Paul's abandonment and spectacular coming-out had been hard on all of them, a terrible shock. But, while she had unravelled like a dropped spool of yarn and Emma, Seb's older sister, had taken refuge in anger and acting out, Seb had held things together with a maturity and stoicism far beyond his years.

'If someone's gay, they're gay,' her son had told her calmly while she sobbed on his shoulders. 'It's not Dad's fault and it's certainly not yours. You just have to, you know, get on with it.'

And Seb had 'got on with it', going back to boarding school with no apparent problems, even spending occasional weekends with his father and his new partner, Mike. When Penny had steeled herself to ask Seb what the boyfriend was like, he'd shrugged and said simply, 'All right. He can fix toasters. And he likes cricket.'

For Seb Harwich, the world was divided not into gay and straight, old and young, rich and poor, but into those who did and did not like cricket. How Penny wished her own world-view could be so simple, so accepting.

As it was, she felt guilty about everything. Guilty for not reading the signs, for not knowing about Paul, for not changing him. Guilty for not being a better mother, a better wife, a better artist, a better person. And, while Penny was busy blaming herself, her daughter Emma vociferously seconded the motion, blaming her mother for everything from her father's sexuality, to the dilapidated state of the house, to the weather.

The chicken casserole, Emma's favourite, had been Penny's latest doomed attempt at appeasement. Emma was home for a week, ostensibly to watch Sebby in the big cricket match, but actually to have her photograph taken, bask in male attention and make her poor mother's life as hellish as humanly possible. It was hard to know what, exactly, had pushed Emma Harwich from being a normal, slightly moody teenager, to a full-on-entitled, spoiled bitch. Whether it was the bombshell dropped by her father or the explosion of her modelling career, which had happened at about the same time, Penny didn't know. Either way, it was safe to say that money, fame and attention had not had a beneficial effect on Emma's character.

This was really Seb's big moment, and Penny knew that she should be focusing on her son this week and not her daughter. Not only was it the first time he'd made the team, but Seb would be the youngest player in Swell Valley cricketing history to bat for Fittlescombe against their age-old rivals. As ever, however, Emma was the squeaky wheel that ended up getting the grease.

Seb came back in to find his mother pulling leftovers out of the fridge with the frenzied energy of a bag lady trawling for food in a dustbin. 'What on earth am I going to give her now?' she wailed. 'She only eats chicken and fish.'

'Mum, it's Emma, not the bloody Queen,' said Seb, calmly

putting the food back. 'You've got cheese. Let's have pasta and cheese sauce.'

'She'll never eat that. Far too many calories,' fretted Penny.

'Well she'll have to go hungry, then, won't she?' said Seb. 'We'll do a salad on the side. She can stick to that if she's fussy. But you've got to have the pasta, Mum. You're too thin.'

This was also true. At thirty-nine, Penelope Harwich was still extremely pretty in a wild-haired, hippyish, Pre-Raphaelite-beauty sort of a way. But the stress of divorce had stripped the pounds off her already small frame, to the point where the jut of her hip bones and ribs was clearly visible through the long cotton sundress she was wearing.

Twenty minutes later, with the cheese sauce bubbling on the Aga, the pasta almost done and a hearty-looking salad sitting in a big bowl on the table, Penny had started to relax. Seb pulled a bottle of Chablis out of the fridge and had just opened it, ignoring his mother's protests, when the front door opened and a familiar man's voice rang out through the hall.

'Yoo-hoo! Only me.'

'What does *he* want?' Seb's shoulders stiffened. Penny's son was not a fan of Piers Renton-Chambers, the local Tory MP and self-styled 'family friend'. Seb had no memory of Piers constantly dropping round when they *were* a family. But, since his parents' divorce, he'd become an almost constant visitor, offering Penny help around the house, financial advice and, as he put it, a 'shoulder to cry on'. Seb hoped fervently that Piers's shoulder was the only thing his mother might be crying on. He didn't trust the man an inch.

'Be nice,' hissed Penny, just as Piers walked in. Considered good looking for a politician, at forty Piers Renton-Chambers was probably at the height of his charms. He was reasonably tall and regular-featured, and he still had a full head of hair, although the beginnings of a widow's peak were starting to form, a fact that bothered him quite inordinately. His other attributes were a deep, resonant, orator's voice – no matter what he said, he always sounded slightly as if he were making a speech – and his immaculate grooming. Unlike Penny, who rarely got through a day without wearing at least one stained item of clothing, often forgot to brush her hair and was no stranger to odd socks, Piers never looked anything less than dapper, clean-shaven and altogether beautifully turned out. But, if he was a little vain and pompous, he was also incredibly kind. For all Sebby's misgivings, Penny didn't know how she would have got through the last year without Piers's support. And, despite his obvious affection and attraction for her, he had never made a move or overstepped the line – or at least, not yet.

'Oh, you brought flowers. How lovely,' she beamed, relieving him of a hand-tied bunch of pale-pink peonies. 'And peonies, too, my absolute favourite.'

'Are they?' said Piers.

'You know they are, you twat,' Seb murmured under his breath. Happily, neither of the adults heard him.

'Something smells good.'

'It's cheese,' said Seb in a distinctly churlish tone, earning himself a reproachful look from his mother.

'We're having pasta and cheese sauce,' said Penny, pouring Piers a glass of wine. 'You're very welcome to join us.'

'I'd love to,' he enthused.

Seb rolled his eyes and returned to his Nintendo.

'It's a bit of a scratch lunch, I'm afraid,' said Penny. 'I made a casserole for Emma this morning but I totally forgot it and we had to throw it out.'

Just then, as if summoned by the mention of her name, Emma walked in. Dropping her Balenciaga shoulder bag on the floor like a sack of potatoes, and kicking off her Jimmy Choo gladiator sandals, she strode across the room like a ship in full sail, ignoring both Piers and her mother, grabbed a packet of cigarettes from the kitchen drawer, lit one and proceeded to exhale smoke directly over the saucepan.

'Jesus, what the fuck's that?' she said rudely, wrinkling her nose at the pungent smell of the cheese sauce. 'It smells like boiled socks.'

'It's cheese sauce,' said Seb.

'You know, you really shouldn't speak to your mother like that,' Piers said bravely. 'You're lucky to have a mother who cooks for you, at your age.'

Emma looked at him like something she was having trouble scraping off the bottom of her shoe. 'Fuck off,' she said coolly. 'I'm not eating it.'

'Fine,' said Seb crossly. 'All the more for us. Do you want me to drain the pasta, Mum?'

But Penny was watching Emma fill an enormous wineglass up to the very top with Chablis and start chugging it down like water.

'You must eat something, darling,' she said gently.

'I would if you made something edible,' snapped Emma.

Piers watched the way Emma's lip curled when she spoke to Penny, and saw the fury flashing in her strangely mesmerizing, sludge-green eyes. There was no question that Emma Harwich was wildly, intoxicatingly beautiful. At almost five foot ten, most of which was legs, and with the thick blonde hair of a seventies siren, she reminded him of the blonde icons of his own youth: Farrah Fawcett, or a young Jerry Hall, or Agnetha from Abba. Of course, she was skinnier than those girls. Models were expected to be these days.

16

And her face was harder, more angular. There was nothing soft about Emma, nothing maternal or inviting. Instead, she exuded sexuality and arrogance in almost equal measure. It was not an endearing combination, but Piers could see why it had proved to be a successful one professionally, and no doubt in other ways.

'Seb made a salad,' Penny said meekly. 'Try some of that at least.'

Gracelessly, Emma sat at the table, helping herself to a plate of salad without thanks and before the others had even sat down. A few minutes later, however, they were all eating. The pasta was delicious. Forking it down, silently watching the fractured family dynamic around the table, Piers Renton-Chambers decided he would make a point of spending a lot more time at Woodside Hall.

'I suppose you've heard the news?' he said conversationally to Sebastian. 'Santiago de la Cruz has taken a house in Brockhurst. He'll be playing on Saturday.'

Seb dropped his fork with a clatter. 'Are you joking?'

'No,' said Piers, pleased to have engaged the boy's interest for once. 'It's the talk of the village. He's rented Wheelers Cottage, apparently. Moved in a couple of days ago. I believe there have been one or two sightings of him out and about already.'

'But he's a professional!' said Seb. 'Does Will know?'

'Will?' Piers looked questioningly at Penny, but it was Emma who answered him.

'Will Nutley. He's an old boyfriend of mine, and Fittlescombe's "secret weapon" for this year's match. He's quite a good batsman, apparently.'

'He's an amazing batsman,' said Seb hotly.

'My brother hero-worships him,' said Emma bitchily. 'It's rather sweet.'

'I don't hero-worship him. I like him,' said Seb, looking daggers at his sister. 'And I have no idea what he ever saw in *you*.'

'Hmmm. I can't imagine.' Emma laughed arrogantly. The news that Santiago de la Cruz had moved into the next-door village appeared to have worked wonders on her mood. 'Wheelers Cottage, eh?' she said to no one in particular. 'I might have to take a stroll past there tomorrow. Welcome Mr de la Cruz to the neighbourhood.'

'Didn't you hear what Piers said?' Seb was starting to lose his temper. 'He's bowling for Brockhurst.'

'So?'

'So he's the enemy.'

'Don't be silly, Sebby,' said Emma dismissively. 'It's a game of cricket, not a war.'

Seb Harwich looked at his sister with a withering mixture of pity and contempt. Clearly she understood nothing.

'Well, it's turning into a bit of a war as far as the television networks are concerned,' Piers chimed in. 'Now that de la Cruz is playing, Sky Sports have crawled out of the woodwork with a whopping bid for exclusive coverage.'

'They won't get it, will they?' asked Penny. 'I can't imagine the Swell Valley match not being on BBC Two. It would be like telling the BBC they couldn't cover the Boat Race.'

'They won't push the Beeb out, but they might see off ITV,' said Piers, cheerfully. 'Either way, it's good news for the valley, and the constituency as a whole. Money'll start pouring in now.'

'Yes, but it's not about *money*,' said Seb. 'Only a Brockhurster would think like that.' Piers Renton-Wank-Stain seemed to understand even less about the spirit of cricket than Seb's sister. He was surrounded by Philistines.

'Whatever,' said Emma, sighing dreamily, and already

imagining herself on Santiago de la Cruz's well-muscled arm. 'I think it's wonderful that Santiago's playing.'

'"*Santiago?*" What are you, best friends now?' snorted Seb. 'He won't be interested in you anyway,' he added, slurping up the last of his fusilli. 'You'll only make a fool of yourself, throwing yourself at him.'

'Throwing myself?' Emma tossed back her golden mane and laughed loudly. 'He should be so lucky.'

'He's in his thirties. It's disgusting! He's almost as old as Mum.'

'All right, Seb, that's enough,' said Penny, who didn't like the turn the conversation was taking. She agreed that a playboy like Santiago de la Cruz was the very last thing Emma needed in her life. But she knew her daughter well enough to know that, if she dared to say as much, she might as well be delivering Emma naked and wrapped in a bow into the unsuitable Argentine's bed.

'What about poor Will?' said Seb, getting to his feet to clear away his empty bowl. 'You know he's still in love with you. It's vile the way you keep him hanging.'

'I love Will too,' said Emma, a trace of nostalgia creeping into her voice. 'But it's complicated. Our lives are so different now. *We're* so different.'

'Yeah,' snorted Seb. 'He's nice and you're a total cow.'
He stormed off.

'What's got into him?' Emma asked guilelessly, helping herself to her brother's leftover salad. 'He wasn't this moody and obnoxious the last time I came home.'

'I think,' Piers said tentatively, 'he might be a bit wound up about the match. De la Cruz polling up like this at the last minute might be good for the local economy, but it's not exactly cricket, if you'll pardon the pun. This game means a lot to your brother.'

'How would you know?' Emma shot back rudely. Pushing her plate away, she lit another cigarette. 'You're not family, you know.' She too got down from the table and stalked out of the kitchen.

'I'm sorry.' Penny blushed. 'I know it's been a year. But it's been hard for Emma. She was so close to her dad.'

Piers Renton-Chambers put a hand over Penny's and squeezed, in a slightly more than friendly manner.

'You've nothing to apologize for, my dear. She'll grow out of it. They both will.'

I do so hope so, thought Penny. *And I hope Emma was joking about setting her cap at Santiago de la Cruz.*

With her brother and her besotted ex-boyfriend both playing for Fittlescombe, that really would set the cat among the pigeons.

Later that afternoon, having parked his cheery red Mini Cooper on Brockhurst High Street, Piers Renton-Chambers crossed the street to the village shop with a spring in his step. Piers loved his life as MP for Arundel and South Downs. He'd grown up in West Yorkshire, but this part of the Sussex countryside was so stunning, Piers had had no qualms about moving here. Of course, it also provided the added benefit of being one of the safest Tory seats in England. Barring some spectacular scandal, Piers had landed the closest thing British politics offered to a job for life. All he had to do was fix a few potholes and keep the ladies of the local Conservative Party Association sweet. Piers flattered himself that keeping ladies sweet was one of his key political talents, and he wasn't entirely wrong in that assumption. Unfortunately, it was a different matter when it came to finding a wife.

The Swell Valley was renowned as a home, or second home, for a plethora of England's more attractive and eligible women. One could barely step outside one's door without bumping into a famous actress, model, socialite or heiress and, as the local MP, Piers had a built-in excuse for approaching all of them and engaging them in conversation. Yet for some reason, when it came to asking a woman out for dinner, or 'making a move', as the tabloid writers put it, he found himself hamstrung. Inexplicably, the opposite sex seemed to find Piers's chat-up lines cheesy and his romantic approaches were invariably rebuffed.

Since becoming a regular visitor at Woodside Hall, he'd taken things much, much more slowly. Here, for the first time in years, was a real chance: a chance to make a marriage that would be the envy of all his friends in Westminster and at the Carlton Club. Piers couldn't entirely put his finger on it, but he felt sure that today, in some subtle way, he had advanced his case and improved his chances.

A bell above the door rang as he walked into Upton's Stores. Mrs Upton, the shopkeeper, was chatting to a pretty young brunette whom Piers recognized as Laura Tiverton. Laura was a successful television writer who lived at Briar Cottage in Fittlescombe, who had inexplicably thrown herself away on a piece of local beefcake by the name of Gabriel Baxter. Gabe and Laura's engagement party last week had been the talk of villages for miles around.

'Is he really that ill, then? Shame,' Mrs Upton could be heard saying to Laura.

'I don't know any details. But I saw the local GP making a house call to Furlings yesterday and again today. And he wasn't at church last Sunday. That's the first time he's missed a service in more than ten years.'

Furlings was the 'big house', set on a hill above Fittlescombe with panoramic views of the village, the green and the South Downs beyond. Its master, Rory Flint-Hamilton, was the local lord of the manor. *It must be Rory Flint-Hamilton they're talking about*, thought Piers.

Rory's failing health had been the talk of all the local villages for months now – especially as his daughter and sole heir, Tatiana Flint-Hamilton, was a well-known party girl and all-round tearaway. If Tatiana and her fast crowd of London friends were to move into Furlings when the old man died, who knew what would happen to the grand old estate, never mind the village?

'Has the young Miss been home, then? Tatiana?' Mrs Upton asked.

'Not as far as I know.'

An irritated look crossed Laura Tiverton's face. Laura's path and Tatiana's had crossed last Christmas, when Tatiana had run off into the night with Laura's then boyfriend, a little toad by the name of Daniel Smart. Laura was delighted to be shot of Daniel, but she was not a fan of Tatiana Flint-Hamilton. Few local women were.

'To be honest, I'm not even sure if she's expected for the match.'

'Oh, she must be, surely?' Mrs Upton looked shocked.

Laura shrugged. 'At this rate I doubt whether she *or* her father will be there. Rory's lawyer was up at the house last week. It looks as if he's putting his affairs in order, just in case.'

'Shame,' Mrs Upton said again, stuffing Laura's bread and onions somewhat unceremoniously into a plastic bag. 'Mr Flint-Hamilton's such a lovely man. He's done wonders for the village.'

Piers's ears pricked up. As far as he was concerned, Rory Flint-Hamilton's ill health wasn't a shame at all. Fittlescombe's Lord of the Manor and owner of the most beautiful house in Sussex, if not in England, had presented the cup at the

Fittlescombe–Brockhurst cricket match for the last forty years. Should he be too frail to attend this year, however, Piers had been asked to step in as understudy. What with Santiago de la Cruz playing for Brockhurst, and the surge of media interest that the Argentine's sudden arrival had occasioned, Piers couldn't have picked a better year to step into the limelight. Just the thought of so many famous, influential eyes on him, not to mention the TV exposure it would bring, was enough to put a warm glow into Piers's ambitious politician's heart.

'Hello, Laura.' Walking up to the counter, he gave Laura Tiverton what he hoped was a warm and ingratiating smile. 'Are you looking forward to the big match?'

'Of course,' Laura said politely.

'I hear Gabriel and the Fittlescombe boys are training like demons.'

'I couldn't possibly say,' Laura said archly. 'Not to a Brockhurst man like you, Piers.'

The accusation was technically true. Despite his close association with the Harwich family, and by extension the Fittlescombe team, Piers Renton-Chambers owned a small but perfectly formed Georgian house fronting Brockhurst village green. This officially put him in the enemy camp.

'Nonsense, nonsense!' he blustered. 'As MP for both villages, I'm completely neutral. To be perfectly honest with you,' he added, *sotto voce*, 'I don't really approve of Brockhurst bringing in a professional player like this just days before the match.'

'None of us do,' said Laura, lowering her voice so as not to offend Mrs Upton's village pride. 'It's typical, though. Ever since Charlie Kingham got the Brockhurst captaincy, the whole ethos of the team has changed. All they care about is winning, and at any cost.'

TILLY BAGSHAWE

'Hmm.' Piers nodded conspiratorially. 'This de la Cruz fellow sounds like a thoroughly nasty piece of work to me. Oily, too. I don't know if you saw his Robinson's Barley Water advertisement. The fellow's hair was so slick you could have fried chips in it. Ha ha ha!'

'I'm sorry you thought so.'

Santiago's deep, mellifluous tones rang out through the tiny shop. Laura Tiverton blushed, Mrs Upton coughed nervously and Piers Renton-Chambers felt the blood drain from his face like pus from a boil.

'I say. You really shouldn't sneak up on people like that,' said Piers crossly. 'I'm sorry if I offended you. I thought I was having a private conversation.'

'In a shop?' Santiago looked down his hawklike nose at the MP, his black eyes alight with arrogance, like a glamorous racehorse noticing a mangy, stable-yard dog. In perfectly fitting jeans and a plain white T-shirt that showed off both his athlete's physique and mahogany-brown tan to perfection, Santiago radiated enough glamour to light up Oxford Street. When he broke into his famous, wolfish grin, he was in serious danger of setting Upton's Stores on fire. 'Don't worry.' Santiago clapped Piers on the back, a little too heartily for comfort. 'Luckily for you, I'm not so easily offended.' Turning his attention to the mesmerized shopkeeper, he added, 'I wonder, Mrs Upton, is it possible to buy some of your homemade damson jam? I'm told it's very good.'

Poor Mrs Upton nodded mutely and scurried out to the storeroom. She couldn't have looked more bedazzled if Elvis had just strolled into the building.

Ignoring Piers, who still stood hovering by the counter like a spare part, Santiago turned to Laura.

'I'm so sorry. Did I jump the queue?' he said smoothly. 'You were still shopping.'

'No, I er . . . no, no. I'm all done,' Laura babbled nervously, gazing up at him like a schoolgirl. 'Just a few onions. Ha ha ha! Anyway. Enjoy your damsons. Goodbye!'

'Let me carry your bag to your car at least.' Santiago put a hand on her arm just as she was making an embarrassed dash for the door. 'I couldn't bear to seem impolite to such a beautiful lady.'

He was so perfect, even his hands looked as if they'd been newly manicured. Laura tried hard not to think about where they might have been recently, and all the legions of beautiful female bodies they'd caressed.

'Really, thank you, but I'm fine,' she blurted. 'They're not heavy.'

If Gabe heard that Santiago de la Cruz had been seen in Brockhurst High Street carrying her shopping, he was liable to head straight round to Wheelers Cottage and do something less than sporting with a cricket bat.

'I'll see you later, Piers!' Laura called over her shoulder as she scuttled out.

'Here you are.' Mrs Upton returned, triumphant, with a jar of jam. 'That's the very last of this season's batch.'

Santiago reached into his pocket but the old woman shook her head vigorously. 'No, no,' she insisted. 'That's on the house. Consider it a "welcome to Brockhurst" gift.'

'That's very kind of you,' said Santiago, bestowing a second smile on her. 'I must say,' he added, turning back to poor Piers, 'it is nice to be made so welcome by my fellow villagers.'

And with that he swept out, a lingering waft of Gucci Envy aftershave the only reminder that he'd been there at all.

'Well!' Mrs Upton felt quite unsteady on her feet. 'What do you think of that, Mr Renton-Chambers? Quite the gentleman in the flesh, isn't he?'

'Yes,' said Piers, through gritted teeth. 'Quite.'

He tried to recapture his hopeful, happy feeling of earlier, but found that it was quite gone.

WEDNESDAY

Will Nutley made his way along the woodland path with a spring in his step. He had much to be thankful for. It was a gorgeous day, with shafts of warm, pale sunlight piercing the canopy of oak and silver birch and a thick, heady scent of moss and jasmine and honeysuckle and wild garlic hanging in the air. He wasn't in London, stuck at his desk making dreary phone calls to dreary bankers at his dreary, *dreary* recruitment firm, Martin & Rudd. And, best of all, he was just minutes away from seeing Emma again.

Will Nutley had been in love with Emma Harwich for so long that he could no longer remember a time when his heart hadn't been full of her. He was fifteen when they first met, at Brockhurst Manor, the local co-ed boarding school. Emma was only eleven then, four years below him. But already she had the striking good looks that would go on to make her one of the country's most sought-after models. More importantly, she was fun back in those days. Always laughing, always getting up to mischief, and always adoring of Will, whom she adopted first as a sort of cool older brother, and later as her first real boyfriend. As day pupils in a school where almost everybody boarded, Will and Emma often walked home together, along the very path where Will now strolled, carrying a posy of hand-picked flowers and a heart heavy with hope. Their relationship had been a friendship first. It was, Will told himself, still a friendship now. Surely what had blossomed into romantic love once, years ago, could do so again?

Of course, much had changed since those days. Back then, Will had been one of the stars of Brockhurst Manor – older, cooler, and captain of the cricket team. Although he was not the most handsome boy in the sixth form, scores of Brockhurst girls were in love with him, and wildly envious of Emma Harwich, a lowly fourth-year, for snagging him. And then of course there was the 'package' that he came with. Will's family lived in a stunning Georgian pile on the edge of the village and were known to be vastly wealthy. His mother wore couture clothes and was regularly photographed in *Tatler* and even in the society pages of the national newspapers. His father collected vintage Bentleys and threw shooting parties to which the entire county flocked.

Yes, back then it had been Will who had been the catch.

But, after he went away to university, everything changed. Will tried hard to maintain a long-distance relationship with Emma. But she began spending more and more time up in London, clubbing and generally getting herself noticed as a beauty about town. Inevitably, they grew apart. It wasn't long before modelling scouts started to approach Emma. Soon money, success and attention began rolling towards her like a character-destroying tsunami, just as all three of those things were flooding *out* of Will's life like used bathwater. The Nutley family fortune, which had taken a century to build, was lost in a matter of weeks. Will had been forced to drop out of uni and take a job that he loathed in London. With his father on the brink of a nervous breakdown, his mother drinking and his own hopes and dreams in tatters, Will had had no time to focus on his girlfriend. And Emma, dazzled by her new life and career, and dealing with family dramas of her own (Paul Harwich's coming out had shocked everyone, but few people more than his own daughter), drifted further and further away.

For Will, one of the hardest parts had been the fact that they had never officially 'broken up'. There was no tearful meeting, no phone call, no long, Dear John letter, spelling out the inevitable. Will had simply opened a newspaper one day and seen a picture of Emma at a film premiere in Leicester Square on the arm of some smarmy Hollywood director. A string of boyfriends followed, all of them richer and handsomer and infinitely more glamorous than Will.

He had dated, too, of course. A girl from the office; the sister of one of his uni friends. But sex with other women only served to remind him of how much more it had meant with Emma. He'd told himself that his move back to the Swell Valley was prompted purely by longing for the countryside and a need to escape London. But in truth it was the pull both of Emma and of their shared past. If they ran into each other in London, they'd be little more than strangers. But here, in Fittlescombe, their roots were intertwined. Here, he felt sure, he could rediscover the old Emma Harwich and win her back.

The woods ended at a half-rotted wooden gate that led directly into Woodside Hall's paddock. Since the divorce, Penny could no longer afford to keep horses, and the field was now a wild meadow of knee-high grasses, dotted with buttercups and dandelions. Will waded through it, brushing off his shirt and running a hand through his hair as he approached the front door. It swung open before he had a chance to knock.

'Will!'

At least Emma's mother seemed pleased to see him. Smiling broadly, her arms thrown open in welcome, she pulled him into the hallway and wrapped him in a heartfelt hug.

'I saw you coming from the study. Since when do you use the front door, silly boy? You know the kitchen's always open.'

'Well, it's been a while,' he blushed. 'I didn't want to assume—'

'Oh, for heaven's sake! You're as good as family,' Penny insisted. She was looking great, Will thought, and far younger than her thirty-nine years, in a short denim skirt and an ancient tie-dyed T-shirt covered in paint splatters. Her hair was tied up in a bun, from which wisps continually escaped and blew into her eyes and mouth, which she kept pushing away with her hands. Will noticed that these were covered in scratches.

'Skittles,' Penny explained, catching him looking. 'I tried to give the stupid animal a worm tablet this morning. She wasn't having it.'

The Harwiches' cat had been old and cantankerous for as long as Will had known the family.

'Are those for Emma?' Penny gestured to the flowers he was clutching. The walk from the village in such hot weather had left them looking distinctly wilted and sorry for themselves. 'Shall I pop them in some water?'

Just then, Emma appeared at the top of the stairs. In tiny shorts and a sleeveless T-shirt with a faded American flag on it, she looked every inch the supermodel, her long limbs as smooth and brown as sticks of caramel. When she saw Will she smiled, then followed it up with a belligerent glare at her mother.

'Why didn't you tell me Will was here?' she barked imperiously.

'He just arrived,' said Penny, choosing to ignore her daughter's rude tone. 'He brought you some flowers. Isn't that lovely of him?'

'Yes, I can see that. I have eyes,' Emma snapped.

Will felt awkward, witnessing the obvious tension between mother and daughter. But his discomfiture was outweighed by the sheer rapture of seeing Emma again. When she came downstairs and hugged him tightly, whispering, 'It's *sooooo* good to see you!' in his ear, he almost felt as if he might pass out with happiness.

Penny disappeared into the kitchen to find a jug for the flowers. 'Let's sit outside,' said Emma, grabbing a half-empty packet of Marlboro Lights from the hall table and taking Will by the hand. 'Mum can bring us something to drink and we can catch up in peace.'

He followed her out to two deckchairs, half shaded beneath the boughs of a cherry tree and watched, enchanted, while she lit a cigarette and inhaled deeply.

'I didn't expect to see you till Saturday.' Gazing up at the sky, she blew the smoke out through her lips on perfect rings. 'Shouldn't you be at work?'

'I took a few days off. For training,' said Will.

'*Training!*' Emma's tinkly laugh rang out around the garden. 'You're as bad as Sebby. Anyone would think it was the Olympics, not a sleepy old village cricket match.'

Will shrugged. 'There's no point playing if you don't take it seriously. Especially now that Brockhurst have raised the stakes and brought in a pro.'

'Ah, yes,' Emma smiled. 'So I heard. Santiago.'

Will did not like the way she referred to de la Cruz by his first name, or the way it rolled off her tongue.

'But he's no match for you, surely?'

Will couldn't tell if she was flirting with him or mocking him. He wanted so much to believe the former, but it had been so long since they'd spent any time together, he found it hard to read her signals.

'He's a pretty handy fast bowler,' Will admitted. 'Not as good as he thinks he is, of course. No one could be as good as Santiago de la Cruz *thinks* he is. The man's so vain he makes Donald Trump look shy.'

Emma laughed, sincerely this time.

'I'll be at the nets this afternoon with Gabe, working on my block shots,' Will went on. 'If you've nothing better to do, you could come down to the green and watch us.'

He'd tried so hard to sound nonchalant, but there was no mistaking the desperate hope in his voice.

From the comfort of her deckchair, Emma looked across at him coolly. She knew his face so well. Those merry amber eyes and the smattering of freckles that seemed to spread out and join together in the summer months, giving the illusion of being a tan until you got really, really close; both brought back memories of a simpler time. It had been a happier time in some ways. But could one ever go back, after so many bridges had been crossed?

Emma couldn't have said whether she was attracted to Will Nutley any more or not. Whether what she felt was a memory – nostalgia – or something more. What she *did* know was that it felt nice to have him here, wanting her, courting her, obviously still as in love with her as the day they parted ways. Will made her feel safe in a way that no one else could.

'I'm not sure what I'm doing later,' she said.

Will's face fell.

'I should be able to make it, though,' said Emma quickly. 'I'll try. Either way, I'll be cheering you on at the match.'

Will smiled, lying back in his chair and stretching out his long legs as Woodside Hall's garden buzzed with life around him. Emma's reaction wasn't everything he'd hoped for. She hadn't swooned and fallen, damsel-like, into his arms. But it was a start.

Less than an hour after Will had gone, Emma had run upstairs, put on some eye make-up, doused herself in her mother's Chanel Cristalle and set off down the lane towards Brockhurst. By the time she reached Wheelers Cottage, a gorgeous, thatched long-house with roses around an ancient wooden front door and a thick, two-hundred-year-old yew hedge along one side of its idyllic garden, her cheeks were pleasantly flushed with exercise and anticipation. A lesser beauty might have been tempted to stop and check her reflection in a pocket mirror or a parked car's window. But Emma Harwich knew she looked a million dollars as she skipped up to the porch and knocked on the door.

'Who is it?' The voice from inside was deep, heavily accented and quite obviously annoyed.

'A neighbour,' Emma shouted cheerfully back. Half of Brockhurst was probably watching her right now from behind twitching flowery curtains, but Emma couldn't have cared less.

'Can you come back later? I'm a little busy right now.'

Ignoring this distinctly unwelcoming response, Emma pushed her thumb down hard on the latch. As she suspected, the door was unlocked. Delighted with her own ingenuity, she stepped into Santiago de la Cruz's flagstoned hallway and closed the door behind her.

Santiago heard the click of the latch from the kitchen. 'What the fuck? Unless you're Tatiana Flint-Hamilton, or someone equally gorgeous, you'd better have a damn good reason for walking in like th—'

The words died on his lips, and the furious scowl furrowing his brow melted into nothing. Standing in front of him was one of the most utterly ravishing girls he had ever seen. Tatiana Flint-Hamilton might be Fittlescombe's only 'celebrity' beauty, but she clearly had some competition on her hands.

Emma grinned. 'Tatiana? Please. She's well past her sell-by date. I'm Emma Harwich.'

Santiago looked her up and down, taking in the full wonder of her figure. Emma effected the same appraisal, sizing up Santiago's physique like a lioness eyeing a particularly juicy gazelle.

Shirtless and barefoot, wearing only a pair of jeans and some sort of religious medallion around his neck, Brockhurst's newest and most famous resident had an open bottle of beer in one hand and a copy of a magazine that looked distinctly pornographic in the other. In Emma's eyes, he could not have looked more divine.

Belatedly, Santiago recovered the power of speech. 'Do I know you from somewhere, Emma Harwich?'

'Possibly my Burberry campaign,' Emma pouted arrogantly. 'I'm a model. Not in the sort of magazines you read, though.'

She nodded towards the *Playboy* in Santiago's hand. But, if she'd hoped to embarrass him, she was disappointed.

'I read all sorts of magazines,' he said smoothly. Putting both the *Playboy* and his beer down on the hall table, he shook Emma's hand. 'But that's not where I know you from.'

'No?' Emma's eyes twinkled.

'Ah!' he clicked his fingers as it came back to him. 'Of course. You're bikini girl.'

'I'm sorry?'

'You live at Woodside Hall, don't you? In Fittlescombe?'

'Yeees,' Emma said warily. 'How do you know that?'

'My bedroom looks directly into your garden. You were sunbathing there yesterday. Topless, as I remember.'

Emma blushed scarlet. 'You were spying on me?'

'Hardly,' Santiago laughed.

'But . . . but . . . our house must be half a mile away.' Emma sounded outraged. 'You must have had a bloody telescope!'

'Binoculars, actually,' said Santiago. 'They were a gift from my sponsors.'

'What the hell for?'

'For bird-watching. You were a bird. I was watching.'

'You pervert!' said Emma.

'On the contrary,' said Santiago. 'I was admiring the view. How was I to know that one of my neighbours was about to provide a free show?'

With difficulty, Emma regained a little of her composure. 'Yes, well, just remember that the next show won't be free. You'll have to earn it.'

'The next show?' Santiago raised an eyebrow.

'That's right. Don't pretend you don't want to see more. Of course, if you prefer cheap thrills, I daresay Tatiana Flint-Hamilton's giving away front-row seats to her raddled old act. I must say, Mr de la Cruz, I'm surprised to hear you setting your sights so low.'

Santiago smiled. This girl was quite something. On the one hand she was wildly confident, ballsy enough to saunter into his house uninvited and come on to him like a heat-seeking missile. On the other, she was insecure enough to feel the need to badmouth other beautiful women. Tatiana Flint-Hamilton may have had any number of unattractive qualities, but at twenty-three the Swell Valley's most admired female resident was certainly neither 'past her sell-by date' nor raddled.

'Are you always this . . . forward?' Santiago chose his words carefully.

'Not always.' Emma's eyes held his. 'Only when I want something.'

For what felt like an age, the sexual tension crackled between them. Santiago broke it first. 'The kitchen's through there,' he said, walking towards the staircase. 'Go and grab yourself a cold drink while I put a shirt on.'

'Don't get dressed on my account,' Emma called after him. Santiago laughed but kept going.

Emma contemplated following him up to the bedroom, but thought better of it. Perhaps there was such a thing as being *too* full on. A few minutes later, the two of them were sitting at the kitchen counter.

Santiago sipped a Diet Coke. He noticed that Emma had poured herself a hefty glass of white wine, despite the early hour, and that she knocked it back like water.

'So,' he asked her. 'As you're being neighbourly, fill me in. Do you live in the valley all the time?'

Emma rolled her eyes. 'Me? God, no. I live in London.'

'A part-time neighbour, then?'

'If you like,' said Emma. 'But I know all there is to know about these villages. I grew up here.'

'In the pretty house. Woodside Hall.' He put on what he wrongly believed to be an upper-class British accent.

Emma giggled.

'Nice place to grow up.'

'Yes. It was.'

Santiago noticed that her eyes took on a distant expression. She seemed sad suddenly.

'And your parents still live there?'

'My mother does.'

Tossing back the last of the wine, Emma set her glass down firmly on the table, as if indicating that the subject was closed. 'But I didn't come here to talk about me. I want to hear it from the horse's mouth.'

'Hear what, exactly?'

'What lured you to Brockhurst.' She pronounced the word *lured* with relish. 'Beyond the chance to play in a sleepy little village cricket match, of course. I assume you realize you're quite the talk of the valley.'

Santiago filled her in on the sponsor who'd made him the offer too good to refuse. 'I can still play for the county, so I ran out of reasons to say no.'

'Were you looking for reasons?'

He shrugged. 'Maybe. I thought life might be a bit too quiet here. But perhaps I was wrong about that.'

'Perhaps you were.'

Hopping down from her own tall kitchen stool, Emma slid in between Santiago's knees as he remained seated on his. As she stood on the floor, her face was exactly level with his. She brought it so close that their lips were almost touching.

'Aren't you going to kiss me?'

The question was whispered, half-mockingly. If she'd been in any doubt that Santiago was attracted to her, a quick glance at his bulging jeans reassured her.

Following her gaze, Santiago stood up and walked to the window. 'Not right now,' he mumbled. 'No.'

He wasn't sure why he was turning her down. Here was a sexy, single, patently available model, offering herself to him on a plate. And yet something about Emma felt off. Beneath her self-assurance, her veneer of sexual confidence, he sensed a desperate neediness. It reminded him of something in himself, something of which he did not wish to be reminded.

Emma, however, seemed unperturbed by his rejection. 'Suit yourself.' She yawned, stretching her arms dramatically, like a cat. 'Just bear in mind that the clock's ticking. I'll be heading back to London on Sunday.'

Walking up behind Santiago, she slipped her arms around his waist, pressing her impossibly lithe, teenage body against his taut, rigid back.

'If you change your mind before then – *when* you change your mind – you know where to find me,' she whispered in his ear. 'I'll see myself out.'

Santiago waited to exhale until he heard his front door close.

What the hell just happened?

In all his years as a player, both of cricket and of women, he didn't think he had ever been so forcefully propositioned by a girl. Never mind such a *young* girl, a stranger. And in his own kitchen! In the middle of the day! He ought to have felt elated. And yet . . .

No. It wasn't right. As gorgeous as Emma Harwich was, she frightened him. He could well imagine what a tigress she would be in bed. But if he bedded her, then what? Would that be the end? Would she see it through with the chutzpah and dump him mercilessly after a one-night stand? Or would she go to the opposite extreme and stalk him for the rest of his days? Santiago could envisage both scenarios, and neither made him feel comfortable.

Maybe I'm losing my touch?

'Whoa. Whoa! Take it easy.'

Penny Harwich tried to relax as Sparky, her barrel-chested

grey mare, danced and bridled beneath her. Usually the horse was deeply docile and placid – the name had been one of Paul Harwich's little jokes when he'd bought her as a thirtieth-birthday present for his wife. But today Penny's own anxieties seemed to be transmitting themselves down through her saddle, and Sparky was behaving as if she had electrodes attached to her knees.

Riding had long been one of Penny's great pleasures in life. It had been a blow after the divorce when she could no longer afford to keep horses, and had had to sell Sparky back to the local riding stables. Luckily, Mrs Nunn, the stables' owner, was a kind soul and fellow divorcee, who had readily agreed to let Penny ride her old mare whenever she felt like it. Cantering over the fields and through the bluebell woods at the back of Woodside Hall was usually an enormous stress-reliever. Today, however, Sparky's antics were doing little to take her mind off Emma.

Emma had set off in search of Santiago de la Cruz at lunch time, in what looked like a deliberate attempt to rile her little brother and to hurt poor, lovesick Will Nutley. That was bad enough. But then she'd returned an hour and a half later with a beaming grin on her face, reeking of alcohol and laughing to herself in a manner that strongly suggested she'd not only found Sussex's newest cricket star but had already succeeded in her mission to seduce him. Penelope had felt a burning need to escape her house and children and ride her troubles away. Sparky's tantrum wasn't helping.

'Back up.' Penny spoke firmly, jabbing her left heel into the mare's side as she reached down and unhooked the gate that led from the fields onto Foxhole Lane, the main Brockhurst-to-Fittlescombe road. Reluctantly, Sparky took a step backwards, expressing her displeasure with a loud fart as the gate swung inwards.

'Well that's not very polite, is it?' chided Penny, as horse and rider emerged onto the lane. Seconds later, leaning forward to pull the gate closed behind them, she let out an almighty scream. A silver Maserati sports car had rounded the corner just at that moment, sending the grey into a frenzy of panic. Sparky reared up, her forelegs pedalling wildly in the air, just millimetres from the metal bars of the gate. It was a miracle that Penny managed to cling onto her mane, rather than plunge headfirst back into the field.

A squealing of brakes prompted a second, wild rear, before at last the horse was calmed. Penny was angry enough before she saw the driver. But when Santiago de la Cruz came sauntering towards her, resplendent and dazzling in full cricket whites, she completely blew a gasket.

'You bloody idiot! You could have killed me.' Gingerly vaulting down from the mare's back, Penny tied her firmly to the gatepost before storming up to Santiago. 'This isn't downtown sodding Buenos Aires, you know. What speed were you doing?'

'About thirty,' Santiago said, deadpan. 'If that.'

'Nonsense!'

He'd been coming over to apologize and check if the rider was all right. But, now that this woman was being so rude and entitled, he felt all his goodwill ebbing away. 'It is a road, you know. Last time I checked, those were designed for cars as well as horses.'

'It's a country lane, not a race track,' snapped Penny. 'You were out of control.'

'On the contrary,' Santiago bit back. 'The only thing out of control was your animal. If you don't know how to ride, you should stick to the riding school. I've never seen such a fat horse rear that high,' he added nastily.

'How dare you insult Sparky!' Aware she sounded faintly ridiculous, defending the honour of a badly behaved, clapped-out old mare that was, indeed, fat, Penny found herself getting angrier than ever. 'It's bad enough that you turn up here to spoil our traditions and . . . and . . . seduce our daughters!'

'Seduce your . . . what? I'm not seducing anyone's daughters.'

'Ha! Not much,' said Penny.

Santiago looked the skinny woman in front of him up and down. In tight, threadbare jodhpurs, with a mud-splattered blue shirt coming untucked at the waist, and long, sweat-curled tendrils of hair escaping from beneath her hard hat, he couldn't quite decide whether she looked wanton or deranged. She had a pretty, angular face, flushed now from anger and exertion, and long arms and legs that she seemed at a loss to know exactly what to do with, like a puppet with tangled strings.

'Perhaps we should start again,' said Santiago, extending his hand. 'I am Santiago de la Cruz.'

'Oh, I know who you are,' said Penny crossly, shaking hands as briefly and perfunctorily as possible.

'This is the part where you tell me *your* name,' said Santiago patiently.

'Penelope Harwich. I believe you met my daughter earlier today. Emma. The one you claim not to have seduced?'

Santiago's eyes widened as the penny dropped. 'That was your daughter? But you look so young—'

'Please.' Penny bristled with hostility. 'You needn't bother trying to flatter me, Mr de la Cruz. I'm old enough to see right through the likes of you, believe me. Even if my daughter isn't.'

Suddenly, Santiago lost his temper. First Emma Harwich

41

turns up on his doorstep uninvited and all but rapes him in his own kitchen. And now her lunatic mother almost kills him on his way to his first Brockhurst training session, and instead of apologizing starts laying into his morals, not to mention his driving.

'The "*likes of*" me?' he shouted at her. 'What the hell does that mean? You know, you might want to take a look at yourself before you start throwing stones at others.'

'Oh might I, indeed?' thundered Penny.

'Yes. You might. You can't control your horse and you can't control your daughter.'

'How *dare* you!' Penny spluttered. But Santiago was on a roll.

'I stopped to see if you needed help, but three crazy mares in one afternoon is too much even for me. I suggest you get your fat horse back to her stable before you kill somebody. Good afternoon.'

He jumped back into his spotless sports car and sped away, leaving Penny staring after him, open-mouthed.

'Of all the arrogant, obnoxious, hypocritical . . .' she muttered darkly as the Maserati pulled out of sight. Sparky, calmly chewing dandelions by the gate, farted loudly for a second time.

'I couldn't have put it better myself,' said Penny.

She hoped more than ever that Fittlescombe proved the doom-mongers wrong and trounced Brockhurst on Saturday. Something told her that Mr de la Cruz was not used to losing. And that a spot of very public humiliation might do him the world of good.

At the Fittlescombe nets, next to the bowling green, Will Nutley was playing appallingly.

'I don't mean to be rude,' said Gabe Baxter. 'But you're

batting like a blind chimp with advanced-stage Parkinson's. What the fuck?'

'Sorry.' Will shielded his eyes against the long rays of the sinking, reddening sun. *Going down in a ball of burning flame. Like my hopes for getting back with Emma.*

On the other side of the bowling green he saw the stooped figure of Harry Hotham, his old headmaster from primary school, heading back towards the village. Harry was retiring next term after twenty years at St Hilda's, to be replaced by some hotshot from a Hampshire prep school, apparently.

Would Will be replaced by another 'hotshot' in Emma's heart?

It was no good. Everything came back to Emma.

'Don't be sorry.' Gabe's irritated voice dragged him back to reality. 'Be less shit. If I can get you out LBW on the third ball, de la Cruz can do it on his first with his eyes shut. You do *want* to beat the shit out of Brockhurst?'

'Of course,' said Will, stung.

George Blythe, Dylan Pritchard Jones, Lionel Green, Tim Wright and the rest of them had paired up in the remaining six sets of cricket nets. As Fittlescombe's best bowler and batsman respectively, Gabe and Will had been practising together. But it was clear that Will's thoughts were elsewhere. It wouldn't take Einstein to figure out where.

'Seb!' Gabe called out across the green to where Seb Harwich, the odd man out, was waiting his turn in the shade of a crab-apple tree. 'Bowl a couple of overs at muppet here, would you, mate? See if you can take his mind off your bloody sister for half a minute. Because I can't.'

Seb ran over, looking about as happy as a fourteen-year-old boy could. He loved it when Gabe Baxter spoke to him like one of the men; when he called him 'mate' and referred to Will Nutley, one of Seb's all-time heroes, as a 'muppet'.

Taking the red leather ball from Gabe, Seb eyed Will wordlessly from the bowlers' end. At school, they joked around all the time during practice, but not here. The Fittlescombe team took things seriously, and silently. Seb acted accordingly.

Rubbing the ball up and down the length of his thigh, until a pale pink stain marked the white cotton of his trousers, he launched into a short, fast run and bowled as straight as he could to Will's middle wicket. Raising a languorous right arm, Will blocked the shot with ease.

'That's more like it,' said Gabe. 'Well done, Seb. You two keep going. I'm off to the pub.'

Once Gabe sloped off, it wasn't long before the others began to follow him. The light was failing, and most of them had been practising solidly for most of the afternoon, anyway. Before long, Seb and Will were the last two men standing.

Will gazed out past the bowling green to the outskirts of the village. The steeple of St Hilda's Church rose up from the rooftops, and Will and Seb both stopped and listened as its ancient bell tolled six times. It was a lovely sound, timeless and peaceful, as much a part of country life as the soft, cooing call of the woodpigeon or the smell of freshly mown grass on the green on a summer's morning. But tonight it made Will sad.

'She's not coming, is she?'

Seb frowned. 'Does it matter?'

'I suppose not. She said she'd try to come, that's all. When I saw her this morning. I was sort of expecting her.'

'Emma says a lot of things she doesn't mean,' said Seb, adding kindly, if not entirely truthfully, 'Look, I'm sure it's not you. You guys are still friends, right?'

Friends. The word sent a shiver down Will's spine.

'Cricket practice isn't exactly Emma's idea of a riveting evening, that's all.'

'I'm not sure it's mine, either,' Will sighed. All of a sudden, the beer garden at The Fox had an appealing ring to it. If he hurried, he could catch the others before George got in the first round. 'Anyway, you're right: what does it matter?' he reassured himself, smiling at Seb. 'She's coming to the match on Saturday. That's the main thing.'

'Oh, yeah, she's coming all right,' grumbled Seb. 'The question is, who will she be cheering for?'

'What do you mean?'

'Well, ever since she heard about you-know-who playing for Brockhurst, she's had stars in her eyes like you wouldn't believe. She went over to his house this afternoon, you know.'

Will looked ashen. 'To de la Cruz's house?'

'I know,' said Seb, mistaking Will's expression for disapproval. 'It's embarrassing. Like some sort of groupie. Anyway, come on.' He threw the cricket ball high in the air and caught it one-handed. 'We came here to practise. Let's practise.'

As tempting as it was to slope off to The Fox and drown his sorrows, Will Nutley pulled the visor down on his helmet, a look of grim determination settling over his usually placid features.

'Fine,' he said to Seb. 'Give it your best shot.'

There was only one thing for it now.

He was simply going to have to annihilate Santiago de la Cruz.

THURSDAY

Penny Harwich checked her reflection in the mirror of the ladies' loo at Capo, the swanky new Italian restaurant in Lewes, feeling faintly absurd.

For one thing she was on a 'date', a ridiculous enough idea in itself at her age and after twenty years of marriage. For another, her date was with Piers Renton-Chambers, a man who, if possible, felt even more awkward in romantic situations than she did. And for a third it was only six o'clock in the evening. The only people Penny knew who knowingly ate their dinner at six o'clock were either children under eight or what her son Seb rather unkindly referred to as 'Reaper-cheaters', i.e. those so elderly and infirm they had to be wheeled to their beds each night before sunset.

In a long, slightly hippyish dark-green dress, with matching dangly jade earrings, Penny had made an effort with her appearance tonight, something else that added to her embarrassment. After her ill-fated run-in with that vile man Santiago de la Cruz yesterday, she'd returned home and dashed straight to the loo for a pee. There she'd looked in the mirror and almost screamed at the red-faced,

46

sweat-smeared, bedraggled harridan she'd seen staring back at her. No wonder Santiago had thought she'd lost her marbles. With her flaky skin and deeply shadowed eyes, weighed down with more bags than Mariah Carey setting off on tour, she looked as if she were about to turn sixty, not forty. Piers had telephoned moments later to ask her out to dinner. Still in shock, Penny had said yes, thereby plunging herself into a second, even deeper layer of panic. She'd spent the rest of the night washing, conditioning, trimming, exfoliating, moisturizing, deep-cleansing and Veeting any hair that had the temerity to appear anywhere on her body, until her skin glowed red and raw and her gums bled from excessive brushing. Then this morning, only marginally calmer, she'd driven herself into Chichester for a haircut and blow-dry that she absolutely couldn't afford, and some new make-up from Bourjois that she'd once read in a magazine was the same stuff as Chanel, just in cheaper packaging.

But now that she was here, looking primped and pretty and with Piers waiting at their painfully early table, she felt foolish and deflated.

This is Piers.

This is me and Piers, eating some spaghetti I could have cooked at home and pretending we're . . . what? Teenagers? Lovers?

Bloody Santiago de la Cruz. Penny blamed him for all of it. She felt a headache coming on, and wished to goodness she were curled up on the sofa at home in front of the telly.

Back at the table, Piers stood up and pulled out her chair as she approached.

'You're back.' He smiled. 'Thank heavens. I started to wonder if you'd done a bunk. I was picturing you shimmying out of the ladies' room window and legging it down Lewes High Street like Zola Budd.'

'Sorry.' Penny immediately felt guilty. She really didn't know why she was making such a big deal out of one simple dinner with Piers, especially after he'd been so kind and made such an effort. It wasn't easy to get a table at Capo at short notice.

Unfortunately, her headache was getting worse. She clutched at her temples.

'Are you all right?' Piers asked.

'I'm fine,' Penny groaned.

'Is it me?'

'No! God, no,' said Penny. 'You mustn't think that. To be honest with you, it's Emma. I know I should let it go, but she just seems to be getting more and more out of control and further and further out of my reach.'

'Do you not think most parents of teenagers feel the same way?' Piers asked kindly.

'Not like this,' said Penny. 'And most eighteen-year-olds aren't earning six-figure salaries and being told how bloody marvellous they are on a daily basis. It doesn't help.'

'No.' Piers nodded understandingly.

'Nor does Santiago de la Cruz.'

They ordered food. Penny's headache persisted, but she did her best to ignore it. Over a large glass of Chianti and a delicious calamari salad, she slowly started to relax and to pour out her anxieties about Emma. How utterly devastated she'd been by her father's defection. And how this had taken the twin forms of intense insecurity, particularly regarding men and sex, and burning anger towards her mother.

'But surely she can't blame you for Paul leaving?' Piers said reasonably.

'She does,' said Penny.

'But . . . he's gay. *He* left *you* for another man, for heaven's sake.'

'Yes. And Emma would say I drove him to it.'

'How? By having a vagina?' asked Piers.

It was the funniest thing Penny had ever heard him say, not to mention the rudest. For the first time all evening she threw back her head and really laughed, then immediately regretted it when the throbbing in her temples returned with a vengeance. *What on earth is wrong with me?*

'You're terribly pretty, you know. When you smile,' said Piers. 'You should try it more often.'

It was a clumsy chat-up line, but Penny appreciated it all the same. For a fleeting moment, she wondered if he might be about to lean over the table and kiss her. But, instead, his slight forward motion turned into a wave towards the waitress.

'Bill, please,' he said briskly. 'You know, I'd be happy to talk to her if you'd like.'

'Emma?' Penny looked at him incredulously.

'Yes. You know, as an older man. It might help.'

Penny tried to imagine anybody Emma was less likely to listen to, or respect, than Piers. Both her children wore their loathing for the only man she'd spent any time with since their father left on their sleeves. Was it possible that Piers hadn't picked up on this hostility? Did he – could he possibly – imagine that Emma would accept him for one split second as a substitute father figure?

'It's a very kind offer,' she said carefully. 'But I don't think it *would* help. In fact, I'm sure it wouldn't.'

'Really?'

He looked crestfallen. But there was no way around it. Any attempt to foist his advice on Emma would end in abject disaster. Blood injuries couldn't be ruled out.

'Really,' Penny said firmly.

'Perhaps I could have a word with the irksome Argie,

then. Get him to back off,' Piers offered helpfully, resting one hand lightly on the small of Penny's back as he escorted her out to the car park.

'Something tells me that wouldn't work, either,' she said with a sigh, climbing into the driver's seat of her battered old Renault Clio. 'But I do appreciate the offer, Piers. Truly. Sometimes I have no idea why you're so kind to me.'

As soon as she said it, she regretted it. It sounded horribly as if she were fishing for a compliment; or, worse, some declaration of Piers's intentions. Perhaps thinking the same thing, Piers cleared his throat awkwardly and leaned in through the window to plant a clumsy kiss on Penny's cheek. 'You'll be all right to get home?' he mumbled, more for something to say than anything.

'Of course,' said Penny blushing. 'Thank you for a lovely dinner.'

In her eagerness to get away, she shot out of the car park far too fast, then promptly got lost in Lewes's complicated one-way system. One of Paul's biggest bugbears in their marriage had been her nonexistent sense of direction. Feeling his invisible vibes of disapproval now, Penny got more and more anxious, turning the wrong way down a one-way street and almost hitting the wall of one of the narrow, cobbled alleys that led out of the old town. By the time she emerged onto Heywoods Lane, the familiar back road to Fittlescombe and the other Swell Valley villages, sweat had soaked through the back of her dress and adrenaline was still coursing unpleasantly through her veins. The headache that had come and gone all evening had now reached epic proportions, as if all the stresses of her family life were trying simultaneously to drill their way out of her cranium.

Suddenly, she began to feel dizzy. She wound down her window for some fresh air, but it didn't seem to help much.

Forcing herself to focus hard on the road, she tried to grip the steering wheel more tightly, but her palms were so sweaty they started sliding around everywhere. Shooting out her right foot in search of the brake pedal, she accidentally hit the accelerator instead, sending the little car jerking forwards like a broken toy. After that, everything happened at lightning speed. She saw another car in the distance, coming towards her. Then, like some awful surrealist nightmare, the hedges on either side of the lane seemed to rear up and enclose her. Penny swerved, and felt the steering wheel slip out of her hands completely. Then everything went black.

From the top of the hill, Santiago de la Cruz watched in shock, then horror, as the little red Renault swerved across the lane for no obvious reason before plunging at some speed into a ditch.

By the time he reached the scene, screeching to halt and leaping out of his Maserati, the driver was already starting to come to. He saw at once who it was, and felt a stab of real fear when he saw how close she'd come to hitting an oak tree. Had she lost control just a second later, she could easily have been killed.

'Mrs Harwich.' He leaned in through the open window, trying to keep his voice steady and reassuring. 'Mrs Harwich, can you hear me?'

Penny opened her eyes. She was still in the car, with her head resting on the dashboard. Bizarrely, the passenger-side airbag had inflated but not the driver's. Instinctively, she put a hand to her temple and felt warm, sticky blood against her fingers. Panic welled up inside her, followed by nausea.

'Let me help you.'

'It's you,' she mumbled drowsily.

'Yes.' Santiago smiled. He did not look or sound the way he had yesterday. In jeans and an open-necked shirt, he looked to have lost all the arrogance and hostility that Penny remembered from their earlier encounter. His voice was no longer angry and disdainful, but gentle and kind and full of concern.

'You're following me,' she joked weakly.

'Someone needs to,' said Santiago. 'You drive like a lunatic. Is anything broken?'

Gingerly, Penny leaned back in her seat, wiggling her toes and fingers and moving her neck slowly from side to side.

'No. I don't think so.'

'Can you move? If I help you out of the car?'

She nodded. The car was at an angle, head down in the ditch that ran along the side of the lane, and with the driver's-side headlight smashed against a young ash tree. There was no way to open the door. Thankfully, Penny was tiny enough to fit through the open window. Once she'd removed her seatbelt, Santiago reached in and scooped her up under the arms, pulling her out onto the grass verge as easily as a child retrieving a rag doll.

She was bruised, but the worst thing was still her head-ache. Her confusion at running into Santiago again only seemed to make it worse. 'What are you doing here?' she asked, frowning. 'Where were you going when you saw me?'

'Never mind that,' said Santiago. 'Where's the nearest hospital? I'll drive you to A & E.'

'There's no need.' Sitting on the grass in the gathering twilight, Penny pressed her fingers over the gash on her forehead. The blood was thick and coagulated enough to tell her that the bleeding had stopped. Barring a few scrapes and bruises, her headache and some wounded pride, she was fine. 'I ought to go home and call the insurers, though. And the AA, to come and pick this up.' She gestured towards the car that was hissing quietly next to them.

'Don't be ridiculous,' Santiago said, very firmly. 'Of course you must go to hospital. Head injuries are no joke, you know.'

'I wasn't joking,' Penny protested meekly. 'It's just that—'

'No more talking. We're going.'

Scooping her up into his arms like Ivanhoe, Santiago marched over to his waiting Maserati, deposited Penny gently into the passenger seat and drove off, before she had a chance to protest. Growing up in Argentina, Santiago had always seen it as part of the man's role to take charge. Latin women expected it, but here in England it was seen as something of a novelty. Some girls objected, but Santiago had found that most appreciated his brand of macho Argentine confidence. Not that he would have changed it, even if they hadn't. Decisiveness, like arrogance, was hard-wired into Santiago de la Cruz's DNA.

'So where's the hospital?' He kept his eyes fixed on the road.

'Chichester,' said Penny. Resistance was clearly futile. 'Go to the A27 and turn right.'

Santiago drove on in silence. Watching him lean back in the seat, completely relaxed, barely moving except for the occasional twitch of a jeans-clad thigh as he gave the car more gas, or flick of the wrist as he changed gear, Penny thought what a good driver he was, and what an awful one she was by comparison. She imagined him on horse-back, as fluid and graceful in the saddle as a ballet dancer; or on ice skates, gliding across a frozen lake, swift and silent and—

'Is something the matter?'

To her profound embarrassment, Penny realized she'd been staring at him. She'd been thinking how glamorous and attractive he must seem in Emma's eyes, how impossible for an impressionable girl her daughter's age to resist. But that wasn't what it looked like.

'I'm fine,' she blushed.

'You're still in shock, I suspect,' said Santiago. 'Do you remember what happened?'

'Not really,' said Penny, glad of a change of subject. 'I remember not feeling well. I had this terrible headache and then I started to feel a bit dizzy and . . . that was it.'

'From the top of the hill it almost looked like you'd fallen asleep at the wheel. Is that possible?'

'No,' Penny assured him.

'Have you been drinking?'

'No!'

Santiago raised a sceptical eyebrow.

'I had one glass of wine,' said Penny defensively. 'I'd been for an early dinner in Lewes. With a friend,' she added, unnecessarily.

'If you say so,' said Santiago. He sounded irritated suddenly. 'I know your daughter is a big drinker, that's all. I thought it might run in the family.'

'What do you mean?' said Penny. The reference to Emma had made her blood run cold.

'Just that she polished off a bottle of Chablis at my place the other afternoon in less time than it took me to change my shirt.'

'She's far too young for you, you know,' Penny blurted out.

'You think so?'

'I know so,' Penny said crossly. 'You're nearly my age. Emma's a child.'

'I wouldn't say that,' said Santiago, keeping his eyes on the road.

'That's because you don't know her,' Penny said icily. 'Please. Can't you pick someone else's heart to break? Emma's incredibly fragile.'

I wouldn't say that, either, thought Santiago. The Emma Harwich who'd barged into his house like a sex-crazed Sherman tank had been anything but fragile. On the other hand, there *was* a certain sadness about her, especially when she'd alluded briefly to her childhood.

'Was she affected by your divorce?' he asked Penny.

The question was so blunt, Penny bristled at first. 'Aren't all children?'

'Probably, yes,' said Santiago. 'I know when my parents split up I thought the world had ended. I cried for months.'

Surprised by such an honest admission, Penny softened. 'It was especially hard for Emma. She adored her father. Worshipped him, really. In many ways she still does. But Paul left us without a backward glance, without any real remorse. And you know, his coming out as gay was a huge shock to her, obviously. To all of us.'

'You really had no idea?' Santiago sounded disbelieving.

'None,' said Penny. 'I know. Pathetic, isn't it?'

'Not at all. What's pathetic is walking out on your family. Poor Emma. She needs a boyfriend who can restore her faith in men.'

Penny gave him a meaningful look. 'Exactly.'

Her meaning couldn't have been clearer: *Not like you.*

Santiago frowned, irritated, but said nothing. They relapsed into uncomfortable silence.

They arrived at the hospital. When Santiago helped Penny out of the car, her legs gave way completely. She collapsed into his arms so suddenly that he nearly dropped her.

'Sorry,' she said again. 'I just . . . I feel so dizzy suddenly.'

A look of anxiety passed across his brooding features like a dark cloud.

'Let's get you to a doctor.'

The emergency room was busy, but when Santiago strode in, demanding attention for Penny, the crowds of patients parted like the Red Sea. There wasn't a nurse on earth who didn't want to help Sussex's gorgeous star player. Penny found herself being examined within moments of arrival.

She described what had happened in the car, and again just now in the hospital car park: the headache, followed by the dizziness, nausea and sweating palms; the strange distortion of her vision.

'We'll do a CAT scan,' said the young female doctor. 'Make sure there's no internal bleeding from the head trauma, and see what's going on in there.'

Santiago looked nervous. 'But you don't think it's anything serious?'

'Not at all,' the doctor said reassuringly.

'What about the headache? And the dizziness? Those came on *before* the bump on her head.'

'Probably just a migraine,' said the doctor. Clearly she wasn't a cricket fan. Turning smilingly to Penny, she added, 'The husbands always worry more than we do, don't they?'

'Oh, he's not my . . .' Penny began. But the doctor had already wandered off to sign the paperwork, leaving her and Santiago alone.

'I'll wait while they do the scan,' he said. 'I don't want you to worry.'

'I'm not worried,' said Penny. 'And you don't need to wait. You've been really kind but I'll be fine on my own.'

'Don't be silly,' Santiago snapped. 'I said I'll wait.'

Penny gave him a curious look. He knew he sounded

angry. The truth was he *was* angry. But he didn't for the life of him know why.

'You'll need someone to drive you home afterwards,' he said, more gently.

'I can call a taxi,' said Penny. But one look at his face told her it was futile to protest. Besides which, she didn't have the energy for an argument. 'I meant what I said about my daughter, you know,' she said. 'If you really want to help, you'll leave her alone.'

Santiago felt his irritation return. 'I *have* left her alone,' he snapped. 'Emma was the one who knocked on *my* door, not the other way around.'

'Yes, but you didn't have to encourage her,' said Penny reproachfully.

'I didn't encourage her!'

'Oh, come on,' said Penny. 'I saw the smile on her face when she got home. You're not seriously trying to tell me that nothing happened between the two of you?'

'Would it matter if I were trying to tell you that?'

Penny shook her head. 'You should be ashamed of your-self. You're a grown man.'

'And your daughter is a grown woman,' said Santiago, finally losing his temper. He was tired of being falsely accused. 'You can stick your head in the sand if you want to, but that's the truth. Emma isn't some innocent little girl, you know. Far from it. The more you try to control her, the more she's going to pull away.'

'Oh, really?' Penny said indignantly. 'So you're doling out the parenting advice now, are you? Unbelievable! Tell me, is there any area of life where you *don't* consider yourself an expert?'

Luckily the doctor returned before the conversation could degenerate further.

'OK, Mrs Harwich. You can come through for your scan now,' she said briskly. 'Follow me.'

It was ten o'clock and fully dark by the time Penny got home. Santiago dropped her off at the gate after an awkward, completely silent journey back to Fittlescombe. *If he doesn't make the England cricket squad, he could try out for the Olympic sulking team*, thought Penny.

A furious Seb opened the door.

'Where the hell have you been? I've been so worried. Why didn't you answer your phone?'

Penny opened her mouth to explain that her battery had died, but Seb hadn't finished.

'The police were here.'

'The police? Why?'

'PC Scott said they'd found your car abandoned in a ditch. Half the county's out looking for you.'

'Oh, God!' Clasping her aching head, Penny pushed past him to the phone in the hallway. Five minutes later, having explained everything to the local constabulary, she sank down wearily on the sofa, too tired even to make herself a cup of tea. All the hospital tests had been clear. It *was* a chronic, fast-onset migraine, nothing more, and probably stress-related. The gash on her head had needed only a couple of stitches.

'Sorry I yelled at you.' Seb came and sat beside her. Having heard her chat with the police, he now knew the bare bones of what had happened. 'I was really scared. I thought something awful had happened.'

Penny put a silent arm around her son's shoulder and squeezed. Thank God for Seb. Not for the first time, she wondered where on earth she'd be without him.

It was at that moment that Emma came downstairs. In a

pair of ancient, striped, flannel pyjamas, and with her hair tied up in a messy bun, she looked about twelve. Penny winced again at the thought of her and Santiago together. He could say what he liked, but Emma *was* a child, in all the ways that really mattered.

'Oh. You're back,' said Emma, a pointed lack of concern in her voice. 'Have you seen my GHD hair straighteners anywhere? They've gone awol.'

'Mum's been to hospital,' Seb said angrily. 'She hurt her head.'

'Doesn't look too serious,' said Emma, giving a perfunctory glance to the dressing on Penny's forehead.

'How would you know?' snarled Seb.

'It isn't serious,' said Penny, praying that the children wouldn't descend into a full-scale argument. She couldn't have stood a shouting match right now. 'I'm fine. Santiago de la Cruz kindly drove me home. Now all I need is some rest.'

At the mention of Santiago, Emma's head jerked back as if she had whiplash.

'Santiago was here?'

'Very briefly. He dropped me at the gate,' said Penny, explaining how Santiago had come across her by chance after the accident and played the Good Samaritan.

'Why didn't you invite him in?' snapped Emma.

'Because, darling, he'd already spent half the night driving me back and forth to hospital,' Penny explained patiently. 'I didn't want to take up any more of his time.'

'He'd be here to see me, not you!' said Emma, the pitch of her voice rising. 'He probably thinks you're stalking him. It's so embarrassing.'

'For pity's sake,' said Penny. 'I crashed the car! I didn't do it on purpose. Santiago simply happened to be driving past when it happened.'

'How convenient,' sneered Emma.

'Not for him!' said Penny. 'Really, Emma, it's not as if we were on a date. He drove me to A & E. He was being kind, that's all.'

'But you didn't even have the decency to ask him in for a drink?'

Penny sighed. 'Like I told you—'

'Oh, forget it!' snapped Emma. 'You are *so* selfish. It doesn't occur to you that maybe *I* might like to see him. Or that *he* might want to see *me*? He probably only bothered to drive you because he knows that you're my mother and he wanted an excuse to drop by.'

'Oh, my God!' Seb stood up. 'Do you ever listen to yourself? You are so unbelievably obnoxious.'

'Children, *please* . . .' Penny clutched her head, longing for nothing more than a cup of cocoa and her bed. Just as the fight between brother and sister was about to escalate into full-scale nuclear war, there was a loud knock on the front door.

'Aha! That'll be him,' said Emma, pulling the elastic band out of her hair to let it tumble loose around her shoulder, and shamelessly undoing the top button of her pyjama shirt. 'I'll get it.'

Pulling open the door, she could barely contain her disappointment.

'Hi,' Will said nervously. 'I know it's a bit late. But I . . . er . . . I wondered if you'd like to come and have a drink, before closing time.'

He'd obviously had a couple of drinks himself, presumably in order to work up enough courage to walk over to Woodside Hall and ask Emma out. Swaying on the doorstep, his red hair looking silver in the moonlight, he seemed shyer and more awkward than ever. Catching sight of him through the drawing-room window, Penny felt her heart lurch. *Poor boy.*

'I missed you at practice the other night,' he stammered.

'Sorry.' Emma yawned dramatically. 'I got a bit caught up.'

Will tried not to wonder with whom. It was cold out on the doorstep, but she hadn't asked him in, and he didn't want to be rude by asking himself. Belatedly he noticed that Emma was already in her pyjamas.

'You're ready for bed.' He blushed. 'I'm an idiot. I should have come earlier.'

'Or called,' said Emma meanly. Her mother spending the entire evening with Santiago de la Cruz had put her in a foul mood.

'Yes. Sorry,' mumbled Will.

'I'm not really up for a drink tonight,' said Emma. 'But thank you for asking.'

She was about to close the door on him. Taking his courage in his hands, Will put an arm out to stop her.

'Tomorrow, then. Spend the day with me.'

'Don't you have practice?' Emma asked. 'Tomorrow's Friday. The day before the big match.'

'We're meeting at the nets at eight, then we have an hour on the pitch at ten. But George wants us all to relax in the afternoon. Too much pressure won't help us, he says.'

'Hmmm,' said Emma, her eyes glazing over. Few things in life bored her more than cricket.

'So will you? Spend the afternoon with me?' Will asked hopefully.

Emma hesitated. She did enjoy being with Will, and the constant, steady ego massage he provided. A day with Will Nutley was the romantic equivalent of curling up by the fire with a blanket and a good book. Unexciting, but at the same

61

time deeply satisfying. And it wasn't as if she had any firm plans – although she had thought about shopping for a dress in Chichester with her friend Lucy Taylor, picking up some-thing new and sexy for Saturday's match . . .

'We can go for a picnic at Wilmington, by the Long Man,' said Will. 'Come on. It'll be fun.'

Oh, what the hell!

'OK,' said Emma. 'Sure. You can pick me up at noon, once you're finished on the green.' And with that she did close the door, returning to the drawing room looking marginally happier.

Penny was on her feet, being helped up to bed by Seb. The phone rang just as she reached the hallway.

'Good grief!' she sighed. This was turning into one of the longest nights of her life. 'Who can that be, calling so late?'

'Leave it,' said Seb. 'Whoever it is, they can wait till morning.'

'I'll get it,' trilled Emma. Oddly, she was starting to feel excited about her picnic plan with Will.

'If it's Piers, tell him I'm fine and I'll ring him in the morning,' Penny called back over her shoulder.

'Eeugh! Piers,' muttered Emma. 'He's such a pest.' Then, picking up the receiver, she answered the phone with a brusqueness that bordered on the outright rude. 'Hello. Who is it?'

Seconds later, all the hostility drained from her face, replaced by a beatific smile.

'Oh, hi! How are you?' From upstairs on the landing, Penny heard Emma's voice change. 'I hear you were quite the hero of the hour with my mother tonight. Yes, yes, she's fine.'

So Santiago had called. Clearly he had no intention of leaving Emma alone. Penny was depressed but not surprised.

He'd shown her a lot of kindness today, but a leopard didn't change its spots. At least not because the gazelle's mother asked it to.

'Do you want me to help you into bed?' Seb asked her. 'Or bring you anything? Maybe a Nurofen?'

'No, thank you, my darling. I'm fine.' Penny kissed him on the cheek.

She crawled under the covers of her former marital bed, still the most comfortable in the world, and turned out the lamp. Through the floor, she could hear the muffled sound of Emma's voice.

'Dinner tomorrow sounds great,' she was saying. 'No, no. I'm totally free.'

'Poor Will,' Penny whispered out loud, half delirious with tiredness. Then at last she fell into a troubled, fitful sleep.

FRIDAY

About twelve miles from Fittlescombe, the Long Man of Wilmington was probably the South Downs' most famous landmark. For generations the two-hundred-foot-tall figure of a man carved into the chalk hillside was believed to be profoundly ancient, of Iron Age or even Neolithic origin. Recently, however, scientists had discovered that the man was probably first carved out in the seventeenth century, a mere four hundred and fifty years ago. The discovery had done little to deter the droves of tourists and walkers who flocked to Wilmington, especially in summer. Luckily, being a local boy, Will knew all the best off-the-beaten-track picnic spots in the area. Laying out his grandmother's huge old tartan blanket in the shade of an ancient, wizened oak, he knew he had found the perfect, private position for his perfect, private afternoon with Emma, without a Lycra-clad walker in sight.

For once it seemed as if everything was in his favour. The weather was glorious, warm but not too hot, with the gentlest of breezes rustling through the tall grass around them as they lay back and gazed up at the cloudless blue sky. Fifty feet down the hill, a tiny brook, one of the many tributaries of the River Swell, rippled away merrily, its fast-running water providing a backing track to the birdsong that filled the air. Emma, of course, looked perfect in a white-crocheted sundress that barely skimmed the tops of her brown thighs, with her long blonde hair rippling over her shoulders and down her back like poured buttermilk. Better yet, she appeared to be in an unusually good mood, complimenting Will on everything from his aftershave to the food, a veritable feast of pork pies, salad, white Kentish cherries, ham and Gruyère quiche and delicious chilled champagne.

'I'm glad we did this,' Emma sighed, rolling over onto her stomach and reaching out for another handful of cherries.

'Me too,' said Will.

'Lying here like this, it's hard to believe we'll both have to be back at work in London on Monday, isn't it?'

'Oh, God!' Will groaned. 'Please let's not think about that.'

He poured them both more champagne, then lay back against the hillside, watching a monarch butterfly swoop gracefully past them. There would never be a better moment to do what he'd come here to do – to tell Emma truthfully how he felt about her, how he'd always felt about her. And yet, even with the buzz of the champagne, he was so nervous that his heart threatened to leap out of his chest.

'How was practice?' Emma asked idly. 'Are you confident about tomorrow?'

I don't care about tomorrow, Will felt like saying. *All I care about is you.*

Aloud he said, 'We're as prepared as we can be. From what I hear, Brockhurst have barely practised at all since they brought de la Cruz into the team. We're hoping pride may come before a fall.'

Emma closed her eyes and let the sun warm her face. She had dinner with Santiago tonight, a real date, and had butterflies in her stomach just thinking about it, although of course she hadn't mentioned this to Will. She'd been worried at first that she might have come on too strong with Santiago in the beginning, and furious when her mother had monopolized him yesterday, drawing attention to herself as she always did. It was the same with all Emma's boyfriends, even Will. They all adored Penny, and banged on and on about how lucky Emma was to have her for a mother. When Santiago had telephoned yesterday to ask how Penny was, Emma had been sure that it was happening again. But then he'd asked her out, and she'd realized that the whole show of concern for her mother had been no more than a ruse to get close to *her*. The relief was immense, and in a strange way it took the pressure off everything, enabling her to enjoy her afternoon with Will far more than she would have done otherwise.

'Listen, Emma. There's something I've been meaning to say.'

Emma's eyes were still closed. She felt Will's hand creep onto her belly and stroke her gently there. It was a possessive gesture, intimate and bizarrely erotic. Combined with the buzz from the champagne, and the soporific warmth of the sun, it felt wonderful. Her pulse quickened.

'I know a lot has changed. And I know it's been years. But the truth is, I love you. I never stopped loving you.'

'Oh, Will.' Reaching up, she stroked his cheek. Unable to hold back any longer, Will leaned down and kissed her on the lips, softly at first, then harder and more hungrily when he felt her respond. Slipping one arm beneath the small of her back, he supported her as she arched up to meet him, returning his kiss with a passion and intensity that was more than he'd hoped for. Did she – could she – feel the same way as he did? Had she been whipsawed these past few days with the same regret, the same longing?

'You know I adore you,' she said, pulling away at last and sitting up, pushing her tangled hair out of her eyes. 'What we had was so special. It was first love.'

Will felt as if someone had dropped an anvil into his chest, not so much breaking his heart, as flattening it to nothing at all.

Had. Was. Emma was using the past tense. Anything that her words left unsaid was eloquently and devastatingly communicated in the expression on her face: sad, loving, nostalgic. *She feels sorry for me.*

'We could have that again,' he pleaded, wishing he didn't sound so desperate.

Emma shook her head. 'We can't, Will. You know that as well as I do. Don't make me the bad guy for saying it. We can't go back.'

'Why not? We're going back now, aren't we? Here. Today.'

'Yes, but this isn't reality,' said Emma. 'This is one lovely, magical week out of our lives. On Monday you go back to work in the City. I fly to Milan for a four-day job with Gucci. The next week I'm in New York. Our lives are moving at such . . . different paces.'

She was trying to be tactful but it was clear what she meant. She was a success. Will was a nobody. She'd outgrown him.

A million comebacks ran through Will's head, a million answers to all her objections:

Milan, New York, London; that was just geography.

They could have their careers and still be together.

They were happier here, in this valley, together, than in any of those places alone.

But of course, Emma wasn't alone. Emma was never alone. There was a queue of rich, handsome, successful men waiting to be with her. It was over. And yet . . . that kiss, the kiss they'd just shared. Surely *that* was real?

Without saying anything, Will kissed her again. And she kissed him back again, just as fervently as before.

'You still want me,' he whispered in her ear. 'I know you do.'

Emma sighed and got to her feet. It was lovely, kissing Will, hearing him reaffirm his love for her. It made her feel safe and happy. But the pleasure was bittersweet. Everything she'd told him was true. A playboy like Santiago de la Cruz, for example, would fit easily into Emma's glamorous, jet-set, fast-paced world. She could bring Santiago to New York. She could never bring Will. Just trying to picture him sipping Cristalle at a VIP table at Pacha NYC or Soho House was like trying to picture Pope Francis stage-side at Spearmint Rhino or her mother rocking out at a Pete Doherty concert. It didn't compute.

'I do love you, Will. But I think we should go home now.' There was a decisiveness to her voice that hadn't been there before. 'Will you drive me back?'

Penny looked up from her sewing table when the front door opened.

'What are you doing back?' she asked Emma, surprised. 'I thought you and Will were spending the afternoon together.'

'We were,' Emma said tersely. 'We had a picnic and then Will dropped me back.'

'So soon?'

Emma shrugged. She didn't look happy.

'Did you have a row?' Penny probed.

'For God's sake! What is this, the Spanish fucking Inquisition?' snapped Emma. 'No, we did not have a row, OK? I'm tired. I have a date with Santiago tonight and I want to take a nap before I start getting ready.'

'No, you don't.' Seb had wandered through from the kitchen, loudly crunching an apple. 'He called earlier. He can't make it.'

'Ha ha. Very funny.' Emma gave her brother a sarcastic glare.

'I'm not joking,' said Seb between bites of his Braeburn. 'Brockhurst are having a team meeting tonight after practice. It's a three-line whip, apparently. Call him yourself if you don't believe me.'

'I will.' Emma smiled thinly. 'You're so pathetic, Sebby. Really. Don't you think you're too old for these sorts of prank?' Marching over to the phone, she dialled Santiago's number theatrically. Penny noticed that she already knew it by heart.

'Hi.' Her voice took on a thick, sultry tone the moment Santiago answered, which made both Penny and Seb wince. 'It's Emma. I forgot what time you said you were picking me up tonight.'

Penny watched as Emma's face froze, then fell, then hardened into a mask of white-hot anger.

'Well, can't you tell them you've got a prior engagement?' There was a pause. Then Emma said, 'I see. Well, it's your loss.' She slammed down the phone.

'Told you,' said Seb.

'Fuck off,' Emma shot back. All of a sudden her eyes lit on Penny, who was in an armchair in the corner. Emma needed a focus for her anger and, as so often recently, her mother provided it. 'What are you looking so damn happy about?'

'Me?' said Penny.

'Of course you,' said Emma. 'You fancy him yourself, don't you? That's why you don't want me to go out with him. You're jealous!'

'Darling, that's ridiculous,' said Penny. Putting down the cushion cover she'd been working on, she got up and tried to put a comforting hand on her daughter's shoulder. But Emma – still shaken from the conflicting emotions of her picnic with Will, and now reeling with disappointment at Santiago's casual rejection, since clearly he thought nothing at all of cancelling their dinner – lashed out. She hadn't intended to push Penny so hard, but the angle at which she caught her, combined with the force of the gesture, sent her mother reeling backwards. Losing her footing on the flagstone floor, Penny slipped and cracked her head hard on the hall table. She cried out in pain.

'What the hell is wrong with you?' Seb yelled at Emma, rushing to their mother's aid. 'She had a fucking concussion yesterday and now you're pushing her around!'

'It was an accident,' said Emma, her own eyes welling up with tears, mostly of shock. In her anger she had wanted to get Penny off her. But she hadn't intended to hurt her. Less than an hour ago, at Wilmington with Will, she'd been so happy. But now, like a spool of yarn unravelling, everything was going horribly wrong. The waters of self-pity lapped around Emma like a cool, comforting pool.

When the phone rang again, Seb snatched it up. 'If that's you, de la Cruz, you can fuck off, OK?'

'Hello, Sebastian. Actually it's Piers Renton-Chambers. I wondered if your mother—'

'And you can fuck off too,' said Sebby, hanging up.

'Who was it?' groaned Penny weakly.

'Piers.'

She let out a horrified wail. 'Piers? Why were you so rude to him?'

'Because he's annoying. Sorry, Mum, but it's not exactly a good time. I've got better things to do right now than talk to bloody Piers, and so have you. He acts like he's part of the family, and he's not.'

For once, Emma agreed with her brother.

The phone immediately rang again. This time Penny snatched it out of Seb's hand.

'I'm so sorry,' she began. 'Seb didn't mean it. We've had a bit of an incident here and . . .' Her voice trailed off. When she spoke again she sounded as if she'd been winded. All the energy and life had been sucked out of her voice like air from a popped balloon. 'Oh. Hi, Paul. Yes, I'm fine, thanks. It was just a prang.'

'Is that Dad?' Emma's face lit up.

Penny passed her the phone and she pressed it to her ear like a magic talisman, disappearing upstairs without a backward glance, still less a word of apology.

'Are you OK, Mum?' Seb asked Penny.

'I'm fine,' said Penny, returning to her seat in the armchair. 'The insurers called your father about the car. He was calling to make sure I was all right, that's all.'

'I didn't mean about Dad. I meant about Emma,' said Seb. 'Why do you put up with it? Why do you let her be such a bitch to you all the time?'

'She doesn't mean it,' Penny said wearily. 'She misses your dad.'

'So do I,' said Seb. 'That doesn't mean I go through life being an epic dick.'

Penny smiled. She did love Seb's turns of phrase. 'No darling. I know it doesn't.'

'I tell you, all this bloody drama. Anyone would have

71

thought it was Emma who was playing the most important match of her life tomorrow, not me. I'm supposed to be Zen-ing out tonight, you know. George said we all need rest and focus.'

He looked so serious when he said this, so adorably earnest, it was a real effort for Penny not to laugh. Instead, she bit her lip and said, 'Well, off you go, then. Go and rest and focus in your room. I'll do supper early so you can get a good night's sleep. But try to stay out of your sister's way, Seb.'

Seb gave a grunt that might have been agreement and sloped off upstairs.

'And, when she's off the phone, you must ring Piers back and apologize!' Penny called after him.

Seb gave a second grunt, the meaning of which was more unequivocal.

Later that night, after a scratch supper of ham, smoked salmon, salad and baked potatoes that Seb had inhaled and Emma had picked at in a desultory manner, Penny went out for a stroll.

Piers had been his usual kind, understanding self when she'd rung him back to apologize for Seb's outburst earlier. But, embarrassingly, Penny realized when they spoke that she'd completely forgotten to let Piers know about the drama of her car accident after their dinner last night. Perhaps she'd imagined it, but he'd sounded distinctly peeved when she'd told him about it, and more concerned about Santiago de la Cruz driving her to Chichester Hospital and running her home afterwards than about what had actually happened.

'I don't trust that fellow, sniffing about,' Piers had said crossly. 'He's got ulterior bloody motives.'

This, of course, was true. Clearly, Santiago was after Emma, although what exactly his motives were was becoming increasingly unclear to Penny. *Something* had happened between them when Emma had gone over to Wheelers Cottage the other day. That much was plain. And Santiago had shamelessly used Penny's injuries yesterday as an excuse to get into Emma's good books and ask her out on a date. But now he'd cancelled that date and seemed to be blowing hot and cold. Admittedly, it was the night before the big match. But instinct told Penny there was more to Santiago's behaviour than a devotion to the Brockhurst team. It was part of some sort of strategy – playing hard to get, perhaps? She felt fearful for Emma, and for herself. The last thing Penny's shattered family needed was to be messed around by another feckless man.

Pulling her thin grey pashmina shawl more tightly around her shoulders, she turned left and continued up the lane towards Brockhurst village. They'd reached that part of high summer when the evenings seemed endless, and twilight stretched into dawn with almost no true darkness in between. Beneath a pale moon, the lane and hedgerows were bathed in a magical blue light and the warmth of the day still clung to the earth. On either side of Penny, fields of tall grass still buzzed and teemed with life. A dragonfly swooping low overhead like a kamikaze pilot made her duck as it flew towards the river, while fat, inebriated bumble bees made their less graceful way alongside her, moving drunkenly from flower to flower, sated on nectar and the endless bounty of summer.

As she reached the outskirts of Brockhurst, past the first little row of farmworkers' cottages with their pretty front gardens crammed with towering hollyhocks and tumbling dog roses, she heard the bells of St Hilda's Church strike eight. Normally Penny loved the sound of church bells ringing, but tonight for some reason they reminded her of Paul. How many times had she and her husband listened to those bells together, strolling along this same lane, feeling blessed to live in such a beautiful place, blessed with their children, with their life? *We were happy*, thought Penny. Except, of course, Paul hadn't been. All those years, all the time she'd felt so safe and secure and content, he'd been living another life. Miserable. Plotting his escape. Even now, more than a year since the bomb dropped, Penny still struggled to take in the enormity of what had happened. Did one ever truly get over something like that?

Angrily, she pressed her shawl to her eyes, wiping away the tears. They weren't only for Paul, but for Emma and Sebby and all that was lost. Stopping by the side of the road to collect herself, she was surprised to find she'd already walked as far as Wheelers Cottage, Santiago de la Cruz's beautiful rented house. With its thatched roof, leaded windows and wisteria-covered façade, it was an iconic property in the village and indeed throughout the valley, prominently featured on postcards and tourist brochures advertising the idyllic Sussex Downs.

Penny saw that a light was on downstairs. Curious to see what the place was like inside, and knowing Santiago was out with the Brockhurst team, she crossed the lane to peer through the sitting-room window. She was only a few feet away when she suddenly jumped out of her skin. Unaware he was being watched, Santiago walked right past the window. Having stooped down to change the DVD in the machine, he walked back over to the sofa. Slumping back down into his seat, he settled back with a bottle of beer and packet of crisps to enjoy his movie.

So there was no team dinner! thought Penny, watching him

from the safety of the shadows. *He lied. Cancelled on poor Emma for no reason.*

She tried to feel angry on Emma's behalf, but instead found herself feeling curious. Why had Santiago stood Emma up? Why bother to go to the trouble of asking her out only to let her down at the last moment? Clearly, he was arrogant and vain and well known for keeping a string of women at his beck and call. Was this just part of his modus operandi as a playboy? Possibly. And yet the man who had pulled Penny out of her car yesterday and shown such concern for her at the hospital hadn't seemed cruel or spiteful. Piers had talked about his having an ulterior motive. No doubt that was true. But there was also something decent, something kind about Santiago, beneath all the bullshit.

At least, Penny thought there was.

Then again, for twenty years, Penny had thought she was married to a straight man who loved her. What did she know?

Feeling tired suddenly, she turned away from Wheelers Cottage window and began the slow walk home.

SATURDAY

Will Nutley opened his eyes and looked at the numbers glowing red on his bedside clock: 5:05 a.m. Closing his eyes again, he slumped back against the pillow and put his hand to his lips. He could still taste Emma's kiss there, still feel the passion and desire with which her body had responded to him. Her words yesterday had told him not to hope. But her lips had conveyed a different message. Will clung to it this morning, like a drowning man grasping a buoy in choppy seas.

He would stick to his original plan. He would play like a god today and annihilate Santiago de la Cruz. He would be a hero to the whole village, snatching victory from the jaws of defeat. Emma, swept up in the euphoria of the moment, would forget her head and listen to her heart.

In her heart, she loves me, Will told himself.

The first ball would be bowled in less than five hours' time.

Less than half a mile away from the modest cottage where Fittlescombe's star batsman was waking up, Rory

Flint-Hamilton was already up and looking out of his bedroom window with a pair of binoculars, gazing across the village green with more than a hint of nostalgia. This would almost certainly be his last Swell Valley cricket match. His doctors had given him up to a year to live, but Rory could feel in his bones that the end was nearer than that. He wouldn't see another summer in this most idyllic of villages, his home of the last seventy years.

A practical man, not given to sentimentality, Rory Flint-Hamilton was not especially afraid of death. Indeed the prospect of joining Vicky, his darling wife whom he'd missed so terribly these past fifteen years, was altogether an appealing one. The anxiety weighing on his chest this morning was all focused on his wayward daughter, Tatiana, and the future of Furlings, the Flint-Hamilton family estate that Rory felt it his sworn duty to protect and preserve. What on earth was going to happen to the place, and to his daughter, when he was gone?

Outside, a soft grey mist rolled gently across the village green and the cricket pitch beyond. Rory watched as old Stan Driscoll, Fittlescombe's arthritic groundsman, emerged from the pavilion and began pacing the ground, searching for any bumps or irregularities in the immaculately manicured grass. It wasn't yet six in the morning, but Stan was taking no chances. The local bookies had all written off Fittlescombe's chances of victory since the contentious addition of Santiago de la Cruz to Brockhurst's First XI. But, win or lose, no one would be able to cast aspersions on the home team's perfectly prepared pitch. Stan's honour, and the reputation of the entire village, depended on their hosting a flawless event.

Leaning against the window in his tattered old Turnbull & Asser dressing gown, Rory Flint-Hamilton smiled as he

77

watched Stan Driscoll shuffle about his work. At a time when the old ways of life seemed under threat from all sides, days like today, the annual village cricket match, provided a much-needed sense of continuity and comfort. Of course, Brockhurst were doing their best to lower the tone, as usual. Their new captain, Charlie Kingham, was a thoroughly disreputable little oik, who seemed hell-bent on turning the Swell Valley match into some sort of commercial, moneymaking circus. Even so, Rory felt confident that there were enough locals prepared to protect the old ways, and preserve the spirit of the great event, even after he was gone.

Rory's one regret was that he couldn't umpire this year, or give out the coveted Swell Valley CC cup. His health was so fragile, with collapses liable to occur suddenly and unexpectedly, and he would be mortified to be the cause of any disruption or embarrassment. Even so, it was a blow to have to hand over the reins to that twit Piers Renton-Chambers. Rory Flint-Hamilton was not a fan of his local MP, or of politicians in general. Even worse, Renton-Chambers was a Brockhurst man. And a horrible rumour had gone around a few months ago that he'd been spotted in The Fox wearing a pair of grey shoes. *Grey shoes!*

Rory shuddered. Piers had better not think of making such an epic *faux pas* today.

Rory Flint-Hamilton had made his peace with dying of cancer, but not with dying of shame.

By nine thirty, Fittlescombe village looked like Wimbledon on Men's Final day. Every street, lane, car park and available field was jammed with cars, and the media had descended on the valley like locusts. To Sky Sports' fury, and the profound disappointment of Charlie Kingham, Brockhurst's captain, who had hoped to profit from brokering a deal between the network and the local council, they had *not* been awarded exclusive television rights. As a result, the match was a media free-for-all, with both television and radio stations, corporate sponsors and private individual cricket fans all fighting one another for the best vantage points. Enterprising villagers with houses overlooking the cricket field had rented out rooms to rich Londoners willing to pay good money for a front-row seat. With a third of the stands reserved for locals, and another, woefully inadequate third cordoned off for the television camera crews and assorted sporting and social press covering the event, seating at the ground itself was at a premium.

Two sloping fields adjoining the cricket pitch and green and providing an excellent view of both – both owned by Rory Flint-Hamilton – now sported a variety of marquees, including two beer tents and a makeshift hospitality centre serving sandwiches, ice creams, homemade cakes and the like, as well as a long row of portaloos. Fittlescombe Village Council had vehemently opposed any sort of corporate sponsorship, but Brockhurst, keen to keep the money flowing, had 'partnered' unofficially with a number of London companies, whose names and logos could be seen on everything from mugs to paper plates to the bottom of the strawberry punnets supplied by an enterprising Brockhurst farmer.

'Anyone would think it was the Cartier bloody Polo,' grumbled Gabe Baxter. Many ordinary villagers, from Brockhurst as well as Fittlescombe, agreed with him. The country had taken this ancient village match to its heart because it was exactly that – a village match, a treasured remnant of a way of life that was all but dead in modern England. No one, least of all the locals, wanted it to lose that old-world charm. But with each passing year, especially as more and more glamorous media types moved to the valley, it was getting harder – as Seb Harwich and his friends would have put it – to 'keep it real'. There was no doubt that Santiago de la Cruz's inclusion in this year's line-up, combined with the Brockhurst captain's mercenary tendencies, had made it even harder.

Even some of the press were complaining. Graham Yates, the local BBC Radio Sussex cricket commentator, and as mild-mannered a man as one could hope to meet in broadcasting, had had to fight off two ITV crews and a deeply irritating woman from *Hello!* magazine in order to secure his usual pitch beside the pavilion. Broadcasting from the back of a sound van, Graham did his best to convey the heady buzz of the pre-match atmosphere.

'Of course, the name on everybody's lips this morning in the glorious surroundings of this South Downs village is that of Sussex star Santiago de la Cruz.' Yates's deep, mellow tones rang out live over the airways. 'Players from both villages are milling around the dressing rooms here, mingling with the local crowds. But there's been no sign so far of de la Cruz. It could be that he's keeping his distance. No doubt he's well aware of some of the bad feeling his selection has caused locally. Plenty of people here, especially in Fittlescombe, feel that professional players shouldn't be allowed at an amateur match like this one. Of course, Brockhurst have argued that the match rules go back for well over a century and make no such stipulation. Players have to be local, and de la Cruz *is* local. But talking to locals

I— Oh, here he is! Santiago de la Cruz is making his way to the pavilion.'

A vision in perfectly crisp cricket whites, which made his smooth olive skin look even darker, and accentuated the perfect, arrogant, predatory lines of his face, Santiago strode across the pitch like a god. Without exception, every female eye turned to gaze at him, with varying degrees of longing. Despite herself, Emma Harwich felt a lurch in the pit of her stomach. She wished she didn't want him so much, but how could one not?

'And there's de la Cruz, shaking hands with George Blythe,' Graham Yates continued. 'Blythe is of course the captain of the Fittlescombe team this year . . . And it looks like . . . yes, they're about to have the toss.'

Slumped in a fold-out chair at the bottom of one of the fields, just a few feet from the boundary behind the score-boards, Emma Harwich listened grumpily to Yates's commentary on her mother's Roberts radio. Penny had secured a brilliant spot from which to watch Sebby, and support Piers, who was now confirmed as the giver of the cup. She'd been too tired to make a picnic last night, so the wicker basket wedged between Emma's chair and her own was stuffed with ready-made Waitrose pies and sandwiches, plus a few plums from the garden and what was left of the Victoria sponge Penny had made last weekend to celebrate Emma's homecoming. At the last minute she'd thought to grab a screw-top bottle of white wine out of the fridge, along with a clutch of plastic glasses. These were intended for lunch, but she was alarmed to see that Emma had already poured herself a large glass. Play hadn't even started yet. Emma's bad mood of yesterday seemed to have intensified this morning into a full-scale sulk. Penny had half expected her to stay at home and boycott the match, perhaps to 'punish' Santiago for cancelling on her last night. But at the last minute she'd wafted downstairs looking utterly ravishing in a diaphanous, pale-green Stella McCartney tea dress, the look spoiled only by the ugly scowl she wore etched on her perfectly made-up face.

'Oh, that's bad luck,' said Penny, her eyes glued to the pitch as the BBC commentator rambled on. 'Brockhurst won the toss. They're going to bat first.'

'I'm not deaf,' snapped Emma.

'That won't do much for poor Will's nerves, having to wait forty overs before he faces Santiago.'

Emma's scowl deepened. She did not want to think about 'poor Will', who managed to make her feel guilty just by existing, or Santiago, who'd looked preposterously handsome this morning, weaving his way through the parked Ferraris and Bentleys before strutting onto the pitch in his gleaming whites. Catching sight of Emma as he approached the pavilion, the bastard had had the temerity to smile and wave at her as if nothing were wrong. As if it were OK to leave her in the lurch for some stupid team powwow. Emma hated herself for feeling so angry and impotent, and for wanting him so much.

'Oh, my goodness, look!' gasped Penny, as the teams spread out over the pitch and the fielders took up their positions. 'George has put Sebby in to bowl first.'

'Who cares?' Emma yawned.

This was too much for Penny. 'I care,' she said crossly. 'And so should you. This is a huge deal for your brother.'

Emma rolled her eyes.

'He's only fourteen,' said Penny, ignoring her. 'The youngest ever player for Fittlescombe, and he's going to bowl the first ball. He's bound to get his picture in the papers after this. He might even get talent-spotted,' she added, excitedly.

'Whoop-de-do,' said Emma, getting to her feet. 'I'm going for a walk.'

The moment she stood up, half the cameras pitch-side swivelled to look at her. One of the few strokes of good luck Emma had had in recent days was the news that Tatiana Flint-Hamilton, her only real rival for top billing as 'most photographable girl' at today's event had decided to swan off to Sardinia instead, leaving the limelight entirely to Emma. Ignoring the groans and catcalls of 'sit down' from spectators around her, she made no effort to speed up her walk as she sauntered sexily towards the hospitality tent, revelling in the attention. In all the high emotion of the past week, with Will and Santiago and her increasingly fraught relations with her mother, Emma had almost forgotten why she'd come home in the first place. If Sebby did make the papers as opening bowler, he wasn't going to be the only member of the Harwich family to do so.

At first the pace of the match was fast. Seb Harwich, riddled with nerves, made a hash of his first two overs, allowing Brockhurst's openers to score two fours and a six before they'd been on the pitch fifteen minutes. But, as the morning wore on, things settled down. To Fittlescombe's unconcealed delight, Charlie Kingham, Brockhurst's odious captain, was caught out by their harmless church organist Frank Bannister. Despite this, by the time Harry Hotham, one of the umpires, called a break for lunch, Brockhurst had racked up a creditable but by no means unbeatable 282 for 6. Two of their wickets had fallen LBW to an ecstatic Seb Harwich and another player had been caught leg-side by Will Nutley off the bowling of Tim Wright.

This being a village match, the players, spectators and press all ate lunch together in the large hospitality tent in Gabe Baxter's field. A hand-drawn sign outside the marquee announced that neither cameras nor microphones were allowed inside, so that the players could relax and unwind. With Fittlescombe in to bat immediately after lunch, however, there could be no relaxing for Will Nutley. Thirsty after the morning's efforts – by noon the sun was blistering down at close to ninety degrees – he drank two large pint glasses of lemon barley water, but even the thought of food made him feel nauseous.

'You must eat something.' Penny Harwich appeared at his shoulder by the buffet table. Her own plate was piled high with coronation chicken, potato salad and an enormous tomato stuffed with rice. Will wondered how on earth she managed to stay so rail-thin, then thought about how stressful it must have been for her when Emma and Seb's dad pushed off, answering his own question. 'Terrific catch, by the way. Poor old Johnny Usbourne! He looked as if he'd swallowed a wasp, walking off the field.'

'Thanks.' Will smiled. 'I was lucky, though. It was a great ball from Tim.'

He's always so self-effacing, thought Penny, putting two bread rolls on Will's plate despite his protests. *He never takes credit for anything.*

As she thought it, she overheard Piers Renton-Chambers regaling Laura Tiverton with some boring parliamentary story.

'Of course I would never say so myself, but they do say that my maiden speech in the Commons was one of the best in the last century,' Piers boasted. Laura nodded, her eyes glazed. 'But then perhaps that was to be expected. Being president of the Union at Oxford gave me plenty of opportunity to hone my skills as an orator. I doubt making the speech at a village cricket match will be *too* much of a challenge, ha ha ha!'

Penny winced. She knew Piers only talked himself up out of nerves, but it was excruciating to listen to. With his chest puffed out and an incipient double chin wobbling with laughter above his pompous silk cravat, he somehow looked shorter, balder and altogether less attractive than ever. Catching her watching him, he looked up and gave a cheery wave. Penny returned it guiltily. *He's a terribly nice man*, she told herself, like a naughty child repeating a teacher's lines. *I must try to be less shallow*.

Turning back to Will, she was surprised to find he had wandered off. She saw him making a beeline for Emma, who was standing by the Pimm's table on the far side of the room, looking ridiculously lovely, then stopping dead when Santiago de la Cruz approached her.

Both Will and Penny were too far away to hear what was said between the two of them. But the body language, on both sides, spoke volumes. Despite herself, Emma's face had lit up when Santiago came over. When he rested a hand lightly on her shoulder, her whole frame had arched towards him in a ballet of attraction and desire. But then something he said had offended her. Penny watched Santiago's head fall apologetically. Like Will, she saw Emma recoil, as if stung by a bee, then turn haughtily on her heel and stalk off. Unable to stop himself, Will followed her. Penny watched him go, but her eyes kept returning to Santiago, standing where Emma had left him. Running his hands through his thick black hair, he stamped on the ground like a petulant child. He looked both frustrated and exhausted. Like Piers, Santiago sensed Penny watching and looked up suddenly. Unlike with Piers, however, there was no friendliness in his reaction. He stared at her for a moment, frowned deeply, and walked away.

'Mum, there you are!' Sebby came bounding over, as excited and enthusiastic as a Labrador puppy. 'Do you want to come outside and eat with us? Gabe and Laura have picnic chairs and a sun umbrella and everything. George wants to do some last-minute strategizing for our innings, but family members are allowed to join.'

'Of course, darling. Lead the way.'

Penny followed her son out into the sunshine. *This is Seb's day*, she reminded herself, wishing her heart weren't so heavy with anxiety about Emma and her tangled love life.

'Hey.'

Will caught up with Emma outside, under a sycamore tree. She was focusing intently on her phone, apparently reading text messages and typing out hurried, irritated replies.

'Oh, hi. It's you.' Her face and voice both softened a little when she saw him. 'How are you feeling? You're first in to bat, aren't you?'

Will nodded. 'I feel fine,' he lied. He wasn't about to tell Emma how terrified he was of facing Santiago de la Cruz from the bowler's end, or for what reasons. 'Are you having a good day?'

Emma shrugged. 'So-so.' This was a lie, too, and Will knew it. For a moment he stood there just looking at her. She was only feet away from him, yet the distance between them was like a chasm.

Slightly further up the hill, Gabe Baxter and the rest of the Fittlescombe team were lunching together. Emma's brother and mother were with them, although just at that moment Penny stood up and set off back towards the hospitality tent alone. Emma and Will watched her go.

'You should join them, shouldn't you?' said Emma, looking at the others.

'I suppose so.'

'Go on, then.' She kissed him on the cheek. 'I have a couple of calls to make, anyway. I'll see you at tea.' She floated past him like an angel, beautiful but utterly unobtainable – from a different world.

With a heavy heart, Will trudged back up the bank.

'Ah, good, there you are.' Piers grabbed Penny by the elbow just as she was approaching the marquee. She'd come back down in search of Emma, just to check that everything was OK after her run-in with Santiago earlier, but Piers cornered her first. 'Have you seen that daughter of yours? One of the BBC chappies thought it might be a nice idea if we presented the cup together.'

Penny looked blank. 'You and Emma? Why?'

'Well, you know, a pretty face and all that. Two celebrities better than one.'

'*Celebrities?*' Penny giggled. 'You're hardly that, are you?'

Piers didn't appear to see the funny side. 'Emma could hand the cup to me,' he said stiffly. 'Then I could make a little speech and give it to the winning captain. Anyway, have you seen her?'

'No,' said Penny. 'And play's about to restart. I'd better get back to our places. I don't want to miss Seb, or Will.'

'All right,' said Piers. 'I expect she'll turn up at the pitch once Fittlescombe start their innings. Tell her I'm looking for her, would you?'

He scuttled off. Penny realized in that moment with absolute certainly that, whatever her future held, it did not involve Piers Renton-Chambers. Oddly, she felt quite glowing with relief.

Ten minutes later the crowds roared as Fittlescombe came out to bat. Will Nutley and Dylan Pritchard Jones were the opening pair, with Johnny Usbourne bowling the first overs for Brockhurst. Presumably, the idea was to wheel out Santiago de la Cruz later, once Will and his partner had begun to tire, and let the annihilation begin. No one, least of all the event's organizers, wanted to short-change the press by having the home team bowled out before tea. But few doubted the end result would be a whitewash, with a comfortable victory for Brockhurst.

Ignoring the cheers, a grim-faced Will walked out of the pavilion like a World War One soldier about to go over the top. Passing Emma and Penny as he walked onto the field, he was about to acknowledge Emma when he heard her turning on her mother, hissing like a rattlesnake.

'You make me sick!' Emma was snarling. 'You're just an ugly, desperate old slapper. No wonder Dad left. He couldn't stand the sight of you, and nor can I.'

Both her language and her tone were so ugly and violent, Will felt the hairs on his forearms stand on end. As he walked towards his crease, he looked over his shoulder and caught sight of poor Penny Harwich's face. Stricken, mortified and close to tears, she was trying to reason with Emma. But the latter shrieked back at her, her beautiful features contorted with hatred and rage.

For the first time in his life, Will Nutley looked at Emma Harwich and thought, '*You're ugly.*' It was a bizarre feeling, and not a pleasant one, but there was no time to dwell on it. Before Will knew what was happening, Brockhurst estate agent and former number-one bowler Johnny Usbourne was running towards him, hand shielding the ball, eyes narrowed in concentration. Will had caught Johnny out earlier, second ball. It was clear from the bowler's face that he was intent on revenge.

Will gripped the handle of his bat tightly. The battle had recommenced.

CLOSE OF PLAY

Years later, it would be remembered as the most exciting Swell Valley cricket match on record. Fittlescombe's opening pair, Will Nutley and Dylan Pritchard Jones, scored ninety-eight in only ten overs before Dylan was run out controversially just before they reached their century partnership. Will's next three partners, George Blythe, Tim Wright and young Seb Harwich, all went quite cheaply, when the arthritic Frank Bannister, the St Hilda's Church organist, was brought in to bat. There were gasps from the crowd when Brockhurst announced that Frank would be the first Fittlescombe batsman to face the mighty bowling arm of the great Santiago de la Cruz. But, miraculously, the old man survived the two de la Cruz overs he faced before tea, keeping Fittlescombe in the game.

'How do you feel, Santiago?' The press swarmed down on Brockhurst's star bowler like flies on a cowpat before the first cup of Earl Grey was poured. 'Are you embarrassed to be outplayed by a seventy-year-old?'

'Not at all.' Santiago smiled smoothly, affording the reporters an excellent view of his perfectly straight white teeth. 'This is what village cricket is all about. I'm honoured to be a part of it.'

'And what about Will Nutley? How long before you expect his wicket to fall?'

'I have no idea. Let's wait and see, shall we?'

'Do you still anticipate a win?'

Out of the corner of his eye, Santiago saw Penny walking out of the tent. She looked as if she'd been crying.

'Excuse me. I have to go.'

Leaving the press standing open-mouthed by the cucumber sandwiches, Santiago hurried outside after her. 'Are you OK?'

Penny bit her lip, wiping her eyes on her sleeve. 'I'm fine.'

'That's not true,' Santiago said gently. Walking up behind her, he pulled a perfectly pressed handkerchief out of his pocket and handed it to her. Penny took it, blowing her nose loudly before stuffing it into her own pocket. 'Is it Emma? You shouldn't let her walk all over you, you know.'

Penny turned on him. 'Oh? And what should I do? Play hard to get, like you do? Toy with her emotions? Use her?'

Santiago looked at her blankly. 'I'm not playing hard to get.'

'No? Well what *are* you playing at?' Penny sounded utterly exasperated. 'Do you know what she accused me of this afternoon?'

Santiago shook his head.

'Of chasing after *you*. She thinks the reason you stood her up for dinner is because you and I are having an affair! I mean, have you ever heard of anything more ridiculous?'

Santiago looked at the ground. 'This is my fault,' he said quietly.

'At least we can agree on something,' Penny shot back.

'I saw Emma earlier. I told her that she had misunderstood me. That I have no romantic interest in her. She didn't take it well.'

Penny hesitated. This was good news, but she wasn't entirely sure how to react to it.

'Why did you flirt with her when she came over to your cottage the other day?'

'I didn't,' said Santiago bluntly. 'She flirted with me. I tried to shut her down.'

'Well, why did you ask her out for dinner the other night? After the hospital?'

'To talk about you.'

'Me?' Penny looked incredulous.

'Yes. I knew how badly she was treating you, how hurt you were. I called to see how you were doing, and Emma answered. I thought maybe if I talked to Emma privately, I could get through to her. But then, afterwards, I realized how she might misconstrue it as a date. So I made up an excuse and cancelled.'

Penny took this in silently

'So, all this business with Emma . . . was out of concern for me?'

Santiago nodded. 'Concern and . . . something more.' He looked Penny in the eyes. 'Emma got angry with you today because she's jealous. She knows how I feel about you. Of course, you find the idea of the two of us being together ridiculous. It is not so for me. You are very beautiful.'

'I . . . but, I . . .' Penny seemed to have temporarily lost the power of speech. 'I'm far too old for you!' she blurted eventually.

'Nonsense,' said Santiago. 'You are thirty-nine. I am thirty-two.'

'I'm a housewife.'

'So?'

'You're a playboy.'

'Maybe I'm growing up.'

'I can't risk any more maybes,' said Penny, wiping the smile off Santiago's face. 'Not after what happened with Paul. I need certainties.'

Santiago looked at her for a long time. 'There are no certainties. Not with love.'

Kissing her softly on the hand, he walked away.

For at least five minutes, Penny stood rooted to the spot.

Santiago de la Cruz likes me.

He's attracted to me.

He might even be in love with me.

Try as she might, she couldn't reconcile any of the above statements with reality. Wandering aimlessly back towards the cricket pitch, her mind still in a fog of bewildered . . . something . . . *happiness?* – the feeling was so unfamiliar she found it hard to name – she saw Piers Renton-Chambers with Emma, deep in conversation. Then, to her horror, like watching a car crash in slow motion, she saw Piers lean forward and grab her daughter, kissing her forcefully on the lips. Penny opened her mouth to scream, call out, anything, but no sound came out. Instead she watched in silent shock as Emma drew back her leg and kneed Piers hard in the groin. Piers yelped in pain like a castrated dog, before collapsing in a heap on the grass.

'Disgusting old letch,' said Emma, storming off. She walked right past Penny without so much as a glance of acknowledgement, into the open arms of a Channel 4 camera crew, who wanted to interview her about her summer fashion choices.

So that's why Piers spent so much time hanging around the

house, thought Penny, the scales at last falling from her eyes. *It wasn't me he was interested in. It was Emma.*

Had Seb realized it? Was that why he'd been so rude to Piers, so on edge whenever he came over?

And why was it that she, Penny, had no intuition? Never in a million years had it occurred to her that Piers might be after Emma, any more than it had crossed her mind that Santiago de la Cruz might be interested in *her*. Then again, her own husband had been as gay as a maypole for most of his adult life and she'd had no idea about that, either . . .

A voice over the Tannoy announced that play would resume in five minutes. There were only ten overs left, an hour's play at most. Penny longed to go home, lock her bedroom door and lie in a dark room until *any* of this afternoon's events and revelations made sense. But she couldn't leave before the match was over. Seb would never forgive her.

Leaving Piers still writhing around on the grass like a turned-over beetle, she walked back to the side of the pitch in a daze.

Frank Bannister was bowled out the moment play resumed, but after that Santiago de la Cruz's form seemed to crumble utterly. It was bizarre, as if an invisible blindfold had been tied across his eyes, or some awful sudden-onset lethargy had taken over his limbs.

Meanwhile, Will Nutley was playing the game of his life, batting like a man possessed; not for Emma Harwich – after the ugliness he had seen at lunch, Will would never play for Emma again – but for himself. It was a joy to watch. Before long, Penny found herself swept up in the drama of the match, forgetting about Piers and Emma and everything else as she silently willed the home team to win.

The last over of the match began just as the sun was

starting its long, slow slide towards the horizon. At 268 for 8, Fittlescombe needed 15 runs to win off the final 6 balls. Gabe Baxter was in to bat, but it was still Will Nutley, exhausted at more than 150 not out, on whom all Fittlescombe's hopes rested.

You could have heard a pin drop around the pitch as Santiago began the run-up for the first ball. Suddenly, at long last, there it was, the pace and form and pinpoint accuracy that had made him famous. Bringing his right arm down to his side in one perfectly straight, smooth stroke, he released the ball. Bouncing just a few feet from Will and with a lethal top spin, it came within millimetres of the top of his wicket, so fast that Will barely saw a flash of red before it was over.

No run.

The second ball was slower but equally difficult. Will played a straight bat to it, but there was no chance of a run.

At the third ball, desperate to score, he swung out wildly, coming *this* close to taking out his own stumps. Miraculously, however, his bat caught the ball at the right angle, and with enough force to send it high into the air towards the crowd. Aware of Brockhurst fielders running wildly for the catch, Will roared at Gabe and both men started to run. They were still sprinting for dear life when Harry Hotham called, 'Six!'

The crowd were now on their feet. Nine runs to win from three balls. Could they do it?

Gabe was now at the crease, panting like a dog in heat, which didn't help their chances. Laura Tiverton's lone voice shouting, 'Go on, darling!' could be heard as Santiago sprinted towards Gabe. When he thought back on it later, Gabe was pretty sure he had actually closed his eyes as the ball hurtled towards his wicket. But again he heard the glorious sound of leather on willow as he played a beautiful shot, followed by Will's voice. 'Go!' as they scampered three runs.

With two balls to go, Will once again faced Santiago. There was no time to breathe or think or strategize. The great Argentine was running, part ballet dancer, part sprinter, firing off another fast ball like a shell from a cannon. It was in the wicketkeeper's hands before Will had so much as glanced at it.

No run.

The crowd began to stir. Fittlescombe supporters made commiserative noises. Clearly this was going to be Brockhurst's day in the end, but what a close match it had been. Fittlescombe, and Will Nutley in particular, should feel proud.

Santiago prepared to bowl the final ball of the match. Rubbing the ball against his trouser leg, he searched the crowd for Penny Harwich. He'd avoided looking at her up till now, too scared of what he might read in her face.

Penny wanted certainty. Santiago could give her many things, but not that.

He caught her eye and smiled. And, like the sun emerging from the clouds after a dark night of storms, or the snow finally melting after a long cold winter, Penny smiled back.

It was ridiculous, he knew that, but he felt quite delirious with happiness. Practically skipping towards the wicket, he bowled a single, gentle gift of a ball to Will. For a split second confusion registered on Will's face. He couldn't quite believe that de la Cruz had let him off so easily. But then he lifted his bat and swung it wide, a beautiful, graceful arc of a shot that sent the ball pirouetting into the blue sky for a perfect six.

Watching from the pavilion, George Blythe and Tim Wright leaped into each other's arms.

'That's it!' George screamed. 'He's done it! He's bloody done it!'

As crowds of well-wishers surged onto the pitch, Gabe Baxter shook Will's hand. 'Well done, mate. Amazing,' he beamed. 'Emma'll be all over you like a rash now, you wait and see.'

Will looked at him blankly, like a man waking up from a long and confusing dream.

'See?' Gabe winked. 'What did I tell you?'

Will looked up. There was Emma, walking towards him, smiling a confident, knowing, proprietorial smile. Will Nutley was the hero of the hour. And he was hers for the taking. Santiago de la Cruz had sloped off somewhere, to lick his wounds no doubt, but every eye, every camera, was now on Will.

'Darling!' she said, throwing her arms wide and triggering a frenzy of clicking from the paparazzi cameras. But, just as she was about to reach Will's side, another young woman in a smart business suit stepped in front of her, blocking her way.

'Hi, Will. I'm Lisa Dasani from IMG Sports Management. Do you have a moment?'

Will looked at the sports agent. She had red hair, freckles and pale-blue eyes, like a china doll's, and a curvaceous figure practically begging for release from her formal jacket and skirt. She also had the sort of mischievous, one-of-the-boys smile that put him instantly at his ease.

Then he looked at Emma, as perfectly beautiful as a china doll . . . and just as hard and cold. *She's come to claim her prize*, thought Will. *Her consolation prize. Me.*

For a moment he felt a flash of anger, not just with Emma, but with himself. If Emma Harwich had used him, Will Nutley had let her do it. What had his father always said, when he was being bullied at school? 'If you make yourself a doormat, boy, people will walk all over you.'

Will turned back to the pretty sports agent.

'Hello, Lisa.' He grinned. 'Yes, I think I have a moment. Let's go and get a drink, shall we?'

Emma Harwich stood and watched open-mouthed as Will took the redhead's arm and walked away.

He didn't look back.

Penny Harwich had almost reached home by the time Santiago caught up with her.

'You're running away!' he called breathlessly. 'What's the hurry? Didn't you want to see Piers presenting the cup?'

'Not really,' Penny sighed. She told him about the little tableau she'd witnessed earlier, between Piers and Emma.

'Revolting old goat,' said Santiago.

'Yes,' Penny agreed. 'It seems I don't have much of a talent when it comes to judging men's motives.'

'You're too hard on yourself,' said Santiago. 'You're not psychic. None of us are. Sometimes you just have to trust your heart, even if it means taking a risk.'

'And getting burned?' said Penny.

'Perhaps.' Santiago had moved closer, so close that Penny could smell the heady mixture of sweat and aftershave coming off his body, and see the perfect curve of his pectoral muscles beneath his white cricket shirt. *He really is preposterously handsome*, she thought. Next thing she knew, his hands were around her waist.

'And what do you think my motives are?' he whispered, pulling her to him.

Penny's throat went dry. She'd never felt this way with Piers Renton-Chambers, nor even with Paul. 'I wouldn't like to say,' she croaked.

'I'll show you, then, shall I?' said Santiago. 'No more guessing games.'

The kiss went on for a long, long time. Minutes. By the time Penny finally came up for air, the sun had almost completely set, bathing the Downs in a mesmerizing, burned-orange glow.

'Emma's not going to like it,' said Penny, as they walked on together, Santiago's fingers entwined with hers. Nothing had been said, but they both knew where they were going.

'Too bad,' said Santiago robustly. '*You're* going to like it. Trust me on that. I'm going to make you very, very happy.'

'I do trust you,' said Penny.

And, in that perfect, blissful moment, she realized that it was true.

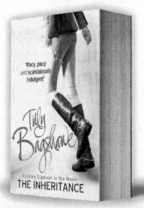

Read more from

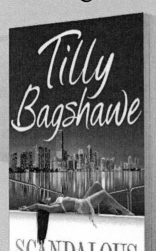

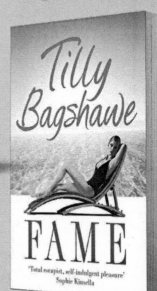

Friends & Rivals

Can you tell them apart?

SCANDALOUS

'Total escapist, self-indulgent pleasure'
Sophie Kinsella

FAME

'Total escapist, self-indulgent pleasure'
Sophie Kinsella

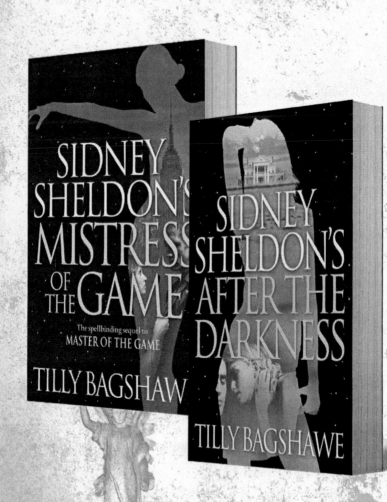

Master storyteller Sidney
through

Sheldon's legacy continues
Tilly Bagshawe

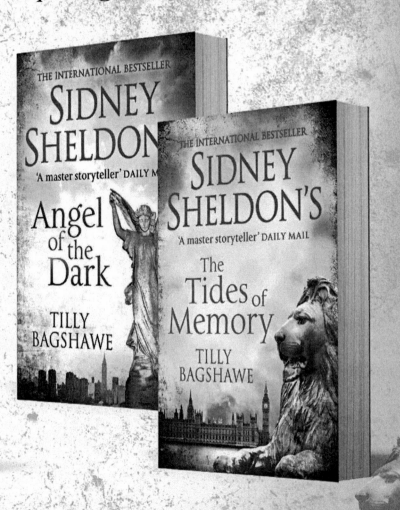

Keep up to date with

www.tillybagshawe.com

Find Tilly on Facebook

 /tillybagshawebooks